RANDI'S STEPS

RANDI'S STEPS

A NOVEL

By Frances Judge

For my husband who I love, who makes me smile, makes me laugh, makes me a better person.

For my parents who have always encouraged me.

2

The silence in Randi's house is loud. On a normal day, the stereo blasts her dad's favorite Billy Joel songs; everyone sings as Randi's younger brother, Michael, hums car noises and screeches his Hot Wheels race car around my feet.

Today, I step into the den across an exclamation point of light shining through the closed curtains. I try to be quiet, but I have to sneeze. An uncontrollable, whistling sneeze. Mr. and Mrs. Picconi look at me. Michael looks at me with his mouth open wide. This must be a stranger's house, not my best friend's.

Did I do something wrong? What happened to "Oh hi, Francie, come on in. You're the next contestant on the Price is Right." Or, "Do you want to get an ice cream cone at Rocket Ship Park?" or "Let's ride in Dad's Corvette and pretend we're movie stars." Why are the Picconis acting stranger than usual, not funny strange—that would be normal—but creepy strange? Did all the towns on Long Island turn weird, or just ours?

Randi appears at the top of the stairs, holding an ice-pack on her head. "I can't play today. My head's about to explode."

"Oh. That stinks." I wait a minute, hoping she's joking. "Well, guess I'll see you at the bus stop tomorrow." I re-zip

11

my coat for the short trek from her front door on Hartwell Drive to mine.

"No, remember? I have to go to the doctor for some tests," Randi reminds me. "Sorry." She turns around, shuffles back into her bedroom, and closes the door. She doesn't say good-bye.

The bright sun is a big fat liar today because the winter air numbs my toes.

This must be her hundredth headache, I've lost count. Shivering from the cold, I step inside.

"You're back already?" Mom says as she takes my coat.

"She can't play because of her stupid headache. Why does she have to go to the doctor for that? She always says she has a headache. Can't she just take some aspirin?"

Dad looks up from his newspaper. "I'm sure it's nothing, but nine-year-olds shouldn't have recurring headaches. She might need glasses. Poor eyesight sometimes causes headaches." He goes back to reading Newsday. A photo of President Carter's serious face replaces Dad's. I peek over the newspaper to see what his eyebrows tell me. He doesn't look concerned, so I'm not concerned.

But mom's green eyes are wide and glossy. "Don't worry about Randi. God is watching over her." She puts down her *Good Housekeeping* magazine and wraps her arms around me, squeezing so hard it hurts. "It's better to see a doctor and

12

find out what is wrong." Mom's voice quivers. And I wonder, *why?*

***

Randi was supposed to be back by now. I hate riding the bus without her. She's been gone over a week for those stupid tests. I miss her Tinker Bell laugh with the occasional snort. The rows behind me bounce with laughter. Spit wads and paper balls land next to me. Missed shots? Should I pretend to read the writing on the seatback in front of me or watch trees go by? I'd love to jump out the window and disappear in the snow.

As soon as the bus rolls down the first hill past the school, bullies and their followers rise like vampires at midnight. A quiet girl like me is high on their list of possible targets, along with the boy wearing coke-bottle glasses, and the chubby Mickey Mouse Fan Club member who carries a metal Mickey lunch box.

Twenty minutes later, the bus inches toward my corner. Way too long.

Mrs. Picconi's station wagon is in their driveway. *Yes!* They're back from the doctor. I leap out of my seat, trip on Joey Torelli's football helmet, and grab my sister who is at the front of the bus laughing with Justin and her second-grade friends.

13

"Come on, Laurie."

"I'm coming," she groans. I run home as fast as I can run through snow and slush with a pile of schoolbooks weighing me down and Laurie screaming, "Wait up!"

"Hi, Mom. Can I go to Randi's? She's back. I saw her car in—"

"Francie, first come here and sit down for a minute. I have to tell you something." Mom reaches for my hand as a tear rolls down her cheek.

3

Randi doesn't need glasses. Randi has cancer. She has a brain tumor that needs to be removed as soon as possible. It's something growing where it shouldn't, like a weed that could spread. I've never known anyone with cancer. I wish I still didn't. What worries me is that she needs an operation on her brain. That definitely sounds serious. *How could I think nothing was wrong? Why didn't I believe her?* The lump in my throat is growing. *Is that how cancer feels?*

"What should I say to her?"

Mom wipes her eyes and wraps her arms around me like a warm blanket. Her silky dark brown hair tickles my shoulders. "Just try to act like you do every day and say you hope she gets better soon."

I drink some milk to wash down the peanut butter cookies Mom made for me, grab my coat, and inch my way over to Randi's, rehearsing the words in my mind. I ring the doorbell and wait, shivering.

Mrs. Picconi opens the door. "Hi, sweetie. Come on in and warm up."

I try to smile as I take my coat off.

"She's on the couch in the den."

Randi looks up at me as I walk in. I forget what I was rehearsing. "Hi" is all that dribbles out.

"Let's go up to my room. I'm sick of this couch."

Randi gathers her pink flowered pillow, a box of tissues, her Paddington Bear, and shuffles down the hall. She looks like she has the flu, not cancer. What does *having cancer* look like, anyway?

I follow her up the carpeted stairs, planting my feet in the indentations of Randi's footsteps. Her hair swings as she climbs, and a cinnamon scent trails behind. *What would it feel like to be Randi? And get the attention she gets?* There is nothing ordinary about Randi—from her beauty to her illness.

We play checkers while we talk.

"You heard I've got cancer? And I have to go to the hospital next week, after Valentine's Day."

I nod. "Do you know how long you'll be there?"

"My doctor says I'll have to stay there for at least a month. I have to have something called radi… radiation treatments every day at first. I can go home when I'm down to three times a week. He also said that my hair is going to fall out." Randi studies herself in the mirror as she pulls her hair back tight enough to raise her eyebrows. "My mom is going to buy me some scarves to wear until it grows back."

What can I say to that? I am in shock. One month seems so long to be in the hospital. Her hair will fall out? *Why, God?*

Randi punches her bed. "I don't want to go. I don't want to go. I don't want to go!" She grabs her bear and throws it

16

across the room, knocking over her jewelry box. We both stare at her handmade jewelry scattered on the rug. "I'm so scared. I want this to stop. Why won't they stop? Why is this happening?"

I don't have an answer, so I bend down and pick up her beaded bracelets. "Maybe I can visit you in the hospital." *Why did I say that?* I hate hospitals.

Hearing a knock at the door, we both flick away our tears. Mrs. Picconi peeks into the room.

"Dinner's ready, Princess. Hurry up before your chicken flies away." Mrs. Picconi flaps her arms a few times and heads back downstairs.

Randi shakes her head and rolls her eyes. "Sometimes she's as weird as my dad."

Mrs. Picconi sounds cheerful, but her eyes have dark circles around them and her shoulders are slumped. I'm usually disappointed when Randi's dinnertime interrupts our games, but not this time. I'm ready to go home.

Twisting back and forth on my cracked plastic swing, my hands freeze on the rusty chain. I keep swinging, numb to the cold, and remember.

We met two years ago when I was eight and she was seven. My family moved next door to her family on Hartwell Drive in a hilly town on Long Island's north shore, a neighborhood overflowing with kids, bikes, and dogs. It was 1976, and it was hot.

I sat hunched over an unpacked box, watching a parade on TV, and sucking a wooden spoon coated with lemon Italian ice from Mario's. Some comedian named Bob Hope told jokes I didn't get as baton twirlers marched behind bands playing "God Bless America." I had to strain my eyes to see anything on the fuzzy black and white screen. Only channel seven came in clear.

The smell of grilled hot dogs and burgers drifted into the den. Everyone celebrated America's 200th birthday. Everyone, but me. Outside, kids I didn't know yet were playing games at the block party while I sat alone—well, almost alone. Laurie lay on the grey speckled rug, scribbling in a Bugs Bunny coloring book and singing a mixed-up version of the ABC song. I wanted to trade places with her. She could be the oldest and handle the friend-making in a new neighborhood while I stayed home and colored.

For three days, I sulked around the house, determined to stay inside for six months until Christmas. On the fourth day of staring at undecorated walls and cardboard boxes, Randi and her mom came over to welcome us.

The first thing Randi said to me was, "I like your name. It rhymes with fancy, and fancy is pretty." From that moment, I liked her. She invited me to her house to play. We became friends on that muggy summer afternoon.

The sweet tasting air transforms into wet snowflakes. I leap off and trudge home, fighting the bitter wind and snow that press against me. The flakes melt on my face, blending with my tears.

I turn the front door knob like a thief trying not to trip the alarm. I want to sneak down the hall and crawl under my covers without being seen or heard. It works until my bed creaks.

"Are you okay, Francie?"

I don't answer. I muffle my crying in the pillow, but those muffled cries are the alarm to Mom. She taps a few times, and the door creaks open.

Mom sits down next to me. "You can talk to me when you need to. I'm proud of you for being a good friend." Mom's voice is soft and she rubs my back.

I sit up and wipe my eyes. "She's gonna be gone a whole month in the hospital." I picture counting the days on a calendar. A month is so long. All I want to do is sleep, wake up tomorrow, and drive away, even on the stupid school bus. Anything to get away from this mess.

4

Another Monday morning of chronic bus-ride-blues. As the wheels turn, so does my stomach. From somewhere behind me, two kids chatter. "Randi missed the bus again…wonder what her excuse is this time. Bet she stubbed her toe."

"Or got a paper cut. 'Mommy, look at this. I can't go to school with a booboo.'"

I strain my neck to see who said it and shout, "Shut up, you jerk!"

Jake and his gang mimic me. My face is burning and my heart races as I clench one fist so tight, nails dig into skin. But I don't have the guts to do what I feel like doing. Instead, I just wish their nightmares would come true. They could show up to school in their underwear or get beat up by bigger eighth grade bullies, or be sucked away by an alien spaceship.

Even though the bus ride was horrible, and I miss Randi, school still beats home today. Nina, sitting next to me, makes me laugh by making silly faces and imitating Mrs. Grayson. I love the slight Spanish accent to her hysterical random comments. "Whoa! You smell that? Who packed the rotten-egg salad for lunch? It's stinkin' up the whole classroom. It's worse than a thousand farts that won't go away!" Uncontrollable giggles give me a stomachache.

Peter who sits next to us doesn't appreciate our humor. He asks to be moved to another table. Julie and her friends are pointing at us from their "cool" table. I wish I could say to them, "I need to laugh. My best friend has cancer on her brain … is going to the hospital … and I won't see her for a month … and my thoughts are so mixed up." But I don't say anything.

Nina turns to me and whispers in my ear. "Guess we scared him away. Hope he remembered to take his egg-farts sandwich with him."

Once again, I cover my mouth to hold in a giggle. *Why doesn't Nina care who stares at us?*

When I take the bus home alone again, I don't feel like giggling anymore. And I don't want to think about Randi's operation. I look up at Randi's window and begin planning my excuses. I'll say I have too much homework. I'll go over to her house tomorrow—or the next day.

I greet Mom with a wave and flip on the TV.

"Hi, honey. Do you want something to hold you over until dinner?" Mom kisses my forehead. If I asked her to bake me a seven-layer cake, I think she would. Mom enjoys applying bandages to scraped knees and serving chicken soup to sore throats. She loves leading the senior citizen club. Her hobby is helping others. I'm not like her.

"Any Ritz Crackers left?" I try to sound as normal as possible. Nothing's bothering me. I'm totally fine.

"Here you go." She hands me a glass of strawberry milk and a plate of Ritz crackers smeared with peanut butter.

"Thanks."

On the couch, I snuggle next to my cat, Oreo, and stroke her shiny black and white fur. She purrs to thank me.

I turn the knob to channel 10 to watch one of my favorite episodes of *The Brady Bunch*. Jan keeps bumping into everything and finds out she needs glasses. I can relate to plain Jan. My eyes are terrible, but I'd rather squint than wear glasses. Mrs. Grayson scolded me once for talking during a quiz. She didn't know that I couldn't read the questions on the board and was asking Nina for help. I never told her why I talked. Then I'd have to wear glasses, and kids might call me Dork or Four-eyes. How will Randi feel wearing scarves and wigs?

Now *Happy Days* is on, and I'm still not doing homework. I ate all the crackers. *Will this show make me happy?*

Dad calls me to dinner. It smells good. Tuna casserole covered in buttery breadcrumbs. While I serve myself, Laurie gets impatient and starts tapping her fork against her empty plate. Each clink bothers me more and more.

"Stop it!"

"You're taking too long. Give me the spoon." Laurie taps even louder.

"Here, you brat!" I throw the spoon at her, sending noodles across the table, onto her shirt and the floor.

Dad loses it. "Francie, go to your room!"

I stomp away, fuming, crying, hungry, and mumbling under my breath. *They always blame me. Just cause I'm the oldest. She started it, and they don't say anything to her.* I stand around the corner, listening to Laurie's loud voice ramble on.

"We had a spelling contest…boys against girls. If you spelled it right you got to put an X or an O on the tic-tac-toe board. I had to spell elephant. Isn't that a hard word? And I got it right! E-l-e-p-h-a-n-t. So I put an O in the middle. Isn't that the best spot?"

"Yes, that's great, honey." Mom's voice is like a whisper compared to Laurie's.

After ten minutes, Dad calls to me, "Francie, you can come out now if you apologize."

I hate to say sorry, but I do since I'm starving.

Laurie keeps talking even with her mouth full. "Justin jumped rope with me today. He said I was the best jump-roper he'd ever seen."

I eat, staring at my plate, not saying a word. Doesn't Laurie know about Randi? Even if she's only in second grade, how can she babble on about a spelling contest and jumping rope?

People say Laurie and I look and sound alike, but we're as opposite as the north and south poles. She's a talker and has lots of friends at school. Nothing ever bothers her.

After dinner, I try to do my homework. I don't care about spelling words right now, and definitely don't feel like doing math. Unless these word problems have the answer to Randi's problem, they're just wasting my time. Who cares how long it takes the Smith family to travel from Utah to Tennessee at a rate of thirty miles per hour?

Randi needs to get home to keep up with her schoolwork. She likes getting straight A's. I like having my friend next door. *Hurry back, Randi.*

5

Randi's bad news has spread around our block. Friends and acquaintances keep calling to ask if it is true. "Does she really have a brain tumor? When does she have to go to the hospital?" My family is sick of answering questions. If it bothers us, Randi's family must want to smash their phone on the floor or bury it in the snow so Frosty can answer it for a while.

Kids are cheering and shouting, so I peek my head out to see. Cold air rushes over my face as I watch their kickball game. I want to join them, be a happy, normal kid again, without worries. How should I act when my best friend has cancer? Do I wait and do nothing until she's better?

Playing outside Randi's house, where she could see me from her window would be wrong, wouldn't it? She might think I'd rather play with other kids who are healthy. I guess I won't play outside until Randi is better. But how long is that?

Maybe she can play indoors. Maybe her head isn't hurting too much, and we can play air hockey and laugh like we did not too long ago. *I have to try.*

Mrs. Picconi opens the door.

"Can Randi play today?" I cross my fingers behind my back.

"Yes, for forty-five minutes. Her head is hurting, but I'm sure she wants to play with you." Randi's mom returns my smile. "Go on upstairs. I'll let you know when time's up."

I rub my fingers along the wooden plaque, tracing the rainbow-colored letters that read *Randi's Room* and knock. This will be the last time I go in her room for a whole month. Or more. I don't want to even think about what I'll do without her.

"Who is it?" Randi's voice sounds muffled.

"It's me."

"Come in …"

When Randi sees me, she sits up in her bed and wipes her nose with a pink tissue.

"Happy Valentine's Day. How's it going?" *Was that wrong to say? Why can't I talk to my best friend?*

"I've been lying around, doing nothing. Here, want my chocolate? It'll get stale while I'm … I'm sick of chocolate anyway."

I take one with caramel oozing out the side, even though I don't feel like eating. "Thanks. I've been bored too."

"I haven't even watched *Tom and Jerry.*" Randi smiles, and we both start to laugh—I have no idea what we're laughing at, but it feels good.

I could never understand why she and Michael love that show so much. Jerry, the mouse, always wins the battle, flattening Tom, the cat, into an accordion shape, or burning his tail off, making a fool out of Tom. I can't see the humor in that, but I laugh when they laugh, like an echo.

We don't talk about the operation, or cancer, or anything sad. I don't even ask her why her pink suitcase is out of the closet.

We play Chinese checkers and braid lanyard key chains from her craft box. My braid is more of a tangled mess of string. I compare mine to Randi's, expecting hers to be perfectly done, but hers is also a twisted mess. We tear them apart and toss the loose strings on our heads. "How do I look with purple hair?" I ask.

"Just divine. How do you like my turquoise hair?" Randi poses for my invisible camera.

"Is that sound coming from Michael's room?"

"Yeah, he's been tossing mini-basketballs at his door hoop since he woke up. He refuses to come out of his room today."

Most days, Michael tags along with us or drags us outside to play baseball. He's like a puppy that hates fences. Sometimes he's a clown. Before I leave and put my shoes back on, I always check them for a plastic bug. He waits to jump out and shout "Got ya!"

He's a lot like his dad. On hot days, Michael and Mr. Picconi shoot me with water guns when I walk into their house. Sometimes I think all the Picconis are bizarre, like every spring when they hold yard-work games …

Last April, before headaches happened, Randi knocked on my door at the crack of dawn. "Guess what? My mom said we could pick up branches around the yard for fifty cents. You wanna help?"

If I were honest, my answer would have been "No. Are you crazy? It's Saturday morning, a perfect day to sleep late, have pancakes, and play baseball." Since I couldn't tell the truth, and she was so excited about this chore, I said, "Sounds like fun. I'll be right out." At least I'd have money for the ice cream man.

When I got outside, Randi, Michael, and their parents were busy shoving sticks in huge leaf bags. They were all smiles, enjoying the "who could pick up the most" contest. What was fun about that? But I played along.

Mr. Picconi judged the size of the bags to decide the winner. I wasn't surprised Michael won. He zoomed around like a roadrunner, stuffing his bag until it was ready to burst. As for me, I couldn't care less how many twigs I collected. I just wanted to finish. The Picconis all looked disappointed that the game was over. Especially Michael.

"Let's do it again, Dad."

"Sorry, all finished. You *crazy* kids didn't miss a stick."

"Aww ... then can you do your Steve Martin imitation for us, pleeeze." Michael begged his dad with his huge puppy eyes.

"Okay, I'm a *wild* and *crazy* guy!" sang Mr. Picconi, shaking his hips and swinging a garbage bag that had branches poking out the bottom.

"Come on in, Wacky. I'll give you *crazy guys* some lemonade." Mrs. Picconi laughed and rustled their hair.

Wacky was the name the Picconis called each other instead of *honey* or *sweetie*. I liked it. Wacky fit.

***

But there is no wackiness in the Picconi's house now. Nothing is funny. *What is going to happen to Randi? Will she be all right?*

Out the window, the charcoal gray sky casts a shadow on Hartwell Drive and hints for me to go home. I don't want to. I don't want to leave Randi's bright pink bedroom. The next time I see her will be in an ugly hospital. Aren't they always pea-green?

We finish braiding our key chains and decide to braid a second one, anything to avoid the good-bye time. But it is too close to ignore. Randi and I are both quiet, waiting to hear her mother's soft steps climbing the stairs to send me home.

31

Now that the sun has set, the busy noises of daytime trickle away. In the twilight hush, we hear Randi's mom reach the top of the stairs. I look at the clock. Exactly forty-five minutes have passed. "Randi, Michael—dinner's ready. You have to say good-bye to Francie." This time Mrs. Picconi doesn't open the bedroom door or joke about flying chicken.

I had been hoping I could leave without saying that word, *good-bye*. What can I say instead? *See you later*, or *have a good night*? I have to say it.

"Bye, I'll miss you."

Randi rubs her sleeve across her eyes. "Bye. I hope you can visit me soon."

We hug, and I leave Randi's room. I'm about to wave to Michael through his cracked-open door, but he is crying on his bed, sobs muffled under his Batman blanket.

Later, in my bed, I have a talk with God …

"Why is this happening to Randi? Isn't she a good person? Is she being punished for the time we embarrassed that girl on the bus—putting scraps of paper on her head and calling them lice? Shouldn't cancer happen to bullies who steal lunch money and tease kids till they cry?

"How did she get this tumor? Is it from something she ate? Did she sleep on one side too much? Was she born with it? Can you make her well the way you healed the sick people in the Bible? Weren't those people Jewish too? Don't you love her?"

Maybe God isn't listening to me now because of bad things I did. I'm sure he saw me cut the hair off Laurie's doll and heard me lie about it. He must hear me groan on the way to church and know I daydream during the service. Maybe I should pray more than the one time a day when I recite the "Our Father" as fast as I can.

Am I too bad for God to answer me?

And if he did answer, how would I even know? Does he speak from the clouds? Send a lightning bolt? I just want to know that Randi will be okay. I need my friend back.

6

The bus rumbles louder and louder down Hartwell Drive. I dash out the front door in my usual panic with Laurie trailing behind me. After finding a seat in the middle, away from Laurie and her chatterbox friends in the front, and away from the wild boys in back, I look out the window to see if Randi left already. Her driveway is empty. My mind rattles with noise from wondering. The trees pass by the window, like dancing silhouettes. I count them to stop thinking.

In class, I try to pay attention to Mrs. Grayson, but I can't. All I can think about is Randi's new room—the hospital room. A hospital is a foreign land to me. I've never even sprained a pinky toe. I imagine the room is painfully dull, not pink and flowery like Randi's room on Hartwell Drive. *What color flowers could I bring to cheer up? Red poppies or ...*

"Francie? Francie, are you with us? I asked you to go to the board to solve problem three. And please put your shoes back on. You're not at Cedar Beach." Mrs. Grayson's face looks the size of a balloon when it's one foot away from mine.

I bend down to slip my shoes back on, but stalling doesn't work. My cheeks glow the color of my imagined flowers. Ignoring the chuckles, I go to the board and answer the problem correctly. The chuckles continue as I slither back and slump into my chair. That lump in my throat is back.

Toward the end of the school day, Mrs. Grayson calls me to her desk. "Is something wrong? You weren't acting like yourself today. I haven't heard you giggling with Nina, and you didn't finish your writing assignment."

This time my words tumble out and tears well up behind my nose. "I'm worried about my friend. She's ... having her brain tumor removed today."

My teacher's deep brown eyes look right through me. Her forehead wrinkles, and she looks surprised with my answer.

"I'm so sorry for your friend. She must be all you can think about today." Mrs. Grayson adjusts the pile of papers she's holding, dropping a few on the floor. "You can have another day to finish your homework."

I return to my seat and wipe my eyes with my sleeve. I'm smiling inside too—an extra day to finish my homework. *How could I think like this? I'm such a jerk.*

At home, Mom stands holding the door open to greet me with a wide smile. "I have good news. Mrs. Picconi called and said that Randi's surgery went better than they expected. They're hoping every bit of the tumor was removed."

It's the best news since the worst news. I hug Mom, not wanting to let go. It's done. Now I can stop worrying and focus on other things.

I am supposed to be rehearsing my four lines for the spring play, *Hansel and Gretel*. Even though I won't be the star, I don't want to mess it up and be laughed at by the entire elementary school.

"Stand tall on stage. Speak loud enough to reach the last row." Mrs. Block reminds me again.

Sure, easy for her to say. My voice cracks when I shout or if I'm nervous. I could teach my cat Oreo to speak before I could change my own voice.

When Nina heard about the play last September, she begged me to try out with her. After her bazillionth time asking, I gave in.

***

Nina and I squeezed our way through the crowd of kids hovering over the cast list. She reached the list first and jumped up and down, announcing that both of our names were there. She was going to be a rabbit, an appropriate part since she was already hopping around. I scrambled to the front and saw my name. "I'm playing … Baby Free?" I was confused, but thrilled at the same time. "I don't remember a baby in *Hansel and Gretel*. Do you?"

"Maybe in this play, Gretel has a little sister. *No problemo*! It will be fun," Nina squealed.

During the week before rehearsals began, I paraded around the house feeling like the queen of showbiz imagining what future roles I might play on TV. I decided I must be good at acting since they chose me for one of the main parts. And someone thought I was cute enough to play a baby.

When our music teacher handed out the scripts at the first rehearsal, I couldn't find Baby Free anywhere. What happened to my starring role? Oh, there it was on page ten. The words Baby *Tree* were joined to my name like a huge pimple on the tip of my nose. Everyone could see I wasn't going to play a cute toddler in a frilly dress. I was going to be a cardboard tree.

Nina burst out laughing at this revelation. "No way! You're a tree wearing diapers! I hope you don't need to be changed in the middle of your scene."

When it was my turn to speak, I ignored Nina's giggles and read my lines like a serious actress. She was getting on my nerves.

"I love snow. I just love it," I rehearsed in my best tree voice, my ego flat as matzo.

***

I may not be the star of the show next month, but practicing has been fun and sometimes I even forget about Randi's troubles.

Randi has been recovering in the intensive care unit for the past three days, and I haven't been able to call her. Lying

37

in a hospital bed doing nothing for that long must be a million times worse than having nothing to do at home. Maybe I can visit soon and bring something to keep her busy. But the idea of seeing the stitches on her head scares me. How will she look after brain surgery?

7

Laurie must be as nervous as I am. I can tell since we're not fighting about something by now. Usually, when she bites her fingernails and hums, I tell her to stop annoying me. And she tells me: You look stupid when you twist your hair. Then I say: You *are* stupid. We go back and forth, ping-pong style, name-calling, until Dad, the referee, threatens to pull the car over, and Mom quotes her favorite command from the Bible: "Love your neighbor as yourself," and explains God means sisters too. This time we both just stare out the window.

My family and I are on our way to Memorial Sloan-Kettering Center in Manhattan to see Randi. It's been three long weeks since Randi had her operation. To cheer her up I'm bringing her some card games, a word puzzle book that comes with an invisible-ink pen, and a jewelry-making kit. My parents picked out a child's bouquet of white mums with red pipe cleaner smiles and googly-eyes tied on to make them happy flowers. They remind me of the talking flower patch from the children's show *The Magic Garden*—except these flowers are quiet.

"You girls know that Randi had to have her head shaved for the surgery. Try not to look surprised," says Dad. "She may be sitting in a wheelchair if she's feeling weak. It was a

39

major operation…she'll need some time to get her strength back."

We both nod our heads. I'm not sure I'm going to like this. I look at Laurie. She isn't smiling. "Your hair looks real nice today."

Laurie's eyes light up. "Thanks. I did the ponytail myself."

"Well, you're getting good at it."

What will I say when I see Randi? How should I act? What if I stare and make her feel like a freak show? Or hurt her feelings?

"Did you hear that?' I lean over the front seat, looking serious. "Sounded like a flat tire."

"No, I didn't hear anything unusual. And how would you know what a flat sounded like anyway?"

"I heard something. We better go back and have the car fixed so it doesn't break down in the city."

"The car's fine. You'll be fine. Stop worrying." Dad winks at me in the rear-view mirror.

"Your dad's right." Mom pats my arm. "Try to stop twisting your hair. You'll get bald spots."

"I know." I sit back and fold my hands on my lap.

Buildings taller than any I've ever seen tower over us now. I can guess that we're almost there. Soaring skyscrapers reflect the cars moving bumper to bumper in walls as shiny as mirrors. Everything seems so overwhelming in New York

City. Streams of people hurry, angry horns honk, intense smells of exhaust fumes and roasted peanuts mix together. It swallows me up. I'm glad we don't live here.

We pass the same Starlite Diner on First Avenue again as Dad circles the block five times, complaining more with each loop. Just when it seems that Dad is going to give up and head home—what I'm hoping for—a spot opens up and he zooms into before it disappears. What's the rush? I'd rather go around the block fifty more times than go into a hospital.

We gather our gifts, get out of the car, and march in silence to the entrance. Where is the children's ward? I feel like a tiny mouse wandering through a huge, sterile maze smelling of beef stew.

Before we reach room 907, Randi's father appears in the hall wearing a doctor's mask and lab coat. "Hello neighbors. Thanks for coming, Just call me Dr. Picconi," he says in a muffled voice.

Laurie and I chuckle at the face drawn on the mask—two goofy eyes and a big nose that moves up and down as he greets Mom and Dad.

"You like my new face?"

We nod.

"Randi likes it too."

Why is he so cheerful? When he hugs me, I smell something stale, like yucky medicine. His shirttail is out and

41

his hair isn't combed. *Did he drive here with the top down in his convertible?*

"Why don't you sit down over there in Mickey Mouse's lobby, and I'll bring Randi out for a change of scenery. I just want to forewarn you—Randi looks a little different right now. She gets sick from her treatments and keeps losing weight…and hair. She chose to have it all shaved off instead of losing it in clumps. But she's excited about seeing you guys."

The lobby is one obnoxious mural. Everywhere I look, I see Mickey Mouse or one of his friends prancing across the walls in bold reds, yellows, and blues. This could become spooky if you stare long enough—too many eyes watching— just like home except cartoon eyes are worse. A few minutes later, I see Mr. Picconi pushing someone else in a wheelchair down the hall toward me.

This isn't my friend, Randi, my friend who could be modeling Macy's dresses. This girl is skinny and pale, without any wavy hair at all. She looks fragile, like a dried leaf, in her wheelchair with tubes attached to her arms. I recognize her smile, but that's it. She reminds me of an injured bird I once saw in our backyard.

I smile back. *Act normal … don't look shocked … act normal. She's still Randi.*

"Hi everybody. Do you like my new hairdo?"

Mom is the first to speak. "It is so good to see you, Randi. We all miss you." She gives her a warm hug. Dad and I follow her example, hugging Randi and telling her how much we miss her. The scene is too much for Laurie to handle.

Dad looks at Laurie's tears streaming down her cheeks. "I'm going to take your sister to the cafeteria and get some ice cream to bring back." He ushers her away. I wish that he'd take me too.

"Oh, good! Bring some back for all of us." Mr. Picconi hands my dad some wadded dollars.

Randi pats her father's belly. "You're getting fat."

"That's okay. Round is good. I'm sure I could float better with extra blubber." As Dad and Laurie reach the elevator, Mr. Picconi calls out to them. "While you're there, look for Rita and Michael. They'll be happy to see you guys." Mr. Picconi takes a step backward and lands with a thump on the grey vinyl chair.

Did he mean to do that?

Randi takes my hand with her tube-free hand and says, "Come follow me … I'll give you a quick tour."

I struggle to look into Randi's eyes and talk as if everything is the same, but I can't trick my mind. Nothing's the same. For the last few weeks and who knows how much longer, this is her home.

"I have the funniest nurse, a male nurse! Sometimes he dresses up like a clown and hands out balloons. He always

43

makes me laugh, telling his silly jokes. Too bad he's not working today—I'd like you to meet him."

Randi introduces us to some other sick kids on her floor and tells me what's wrong with each of them. How can Randi make friends so easily when she's feeling lousy? She even knows the names of all the nurses.

Randi rolls her chair over to the window and I push the IV pole. "Look at this view. Sometimes, when I don't feel like talking to anyone, I sit here and watch the pigeons land on the ledge. I guess what personality each one has and give it a name that fits."

"What would you call that one?" I ask.

"Hmm ... Fred. He looks like the funny one of the flock, doing that wobbly dance."

"You're right. What about that one?"

"I'd call her Danielle the Duchess. She looks like a princess, all shiny, but mean. Did you see her nudge Fred off the ledge? I bet she stares at her reflection all day and steals food from the baby pigeons."

"Yah, I wouldn't want to belong to her flock. But I do like her name—Danielle."

"Me too. I got it from a story one of the evening nurses read."

Looking away from the pigeons and down to the street makes my head spin. "Wow, you could get dizzy from this view! People look like bugs crawling around." Someone tiptoes behind me.

"Boo!" shouts Michael. Mrs. Picconi stands next to him holding two cups of ice cream.

"Would you girls like some?" Mrs. Picconi holds it out to Randi who shakes her head. I love soft vanilla with chocolate sprinkles, so I take it.

"Thanks."

"Here's a napkin. You have to have it at the table over there. We don't want to leave a mess for the janitors. They have so much to clean up already." Mrs. Picconi adjusts Randi's scarf and reties the strings on her hospital gown. After kissing Randi's cheek, she leaves us and joins my mom over by the window. Michael goes in search of more mischief.

We watch our moms. "I think she's tired," Randi says. "She sleeps here on a cot every night. I think my dad's real tired too. He comes here every evening after work. Sometimes he can hardly walk straight."

I can imagine what Mom is saying to Mrs. Picconi— probably something about cancer to get the tears flowing and let her have a good cry. I'd rather talk about anything else, even the bad news that was blasting on the lobby TV about a disaster at the Three Mile Island power plant yesterday. That would be a good conversation starter—is the radiation going to reach Long Island? Is the world going to blow up? Or we could talk about something less explosive, like our favorite pizza. Is plain better than pepperoni? Please, no more talk about this *stupid* disease. No more tears. And please, Mom, no more comforting.

We play card games until Dad announces that it's getting late. He wants to start driving home before rush hour. I feel sad leaving Randi, but I'm glad we're leaving. The hospital smells of stale food, sickness, and sadness.

8

On Saturdays, Mom goes to a pottery class with her friend, Mrs. Torelli, Joey the Quarterback's mother. Laurie and I tag along and paint pre-made statues with Mrs. Torelli's daughter, Isabelle. Since our moms started the class a month ago, Isabelle and I have become friends. We even signed up to take gymnastics class together starting in July. Carpooling to gymnastics with Isabelle will be fun. Her parents drive a Cadillac and always blast the music loud enough to make the car dance.

Since Randi is still away, I've been free to play sports with Isabelle. We play tennis, softball, or gymnastics every day after school. Somehow, I'm having a good time while Randi is in the hospital having the worst time of her life. Wanting to have fun seems wrong, so sometimes I pretend I don't have a sick best friend.

Isabelle lifts a simmering spoonful of sauce from the pot to taste. "Mmm. Mom makes the best homemade spaghetti sauce. 'My nonna's recipe straight from Italy,' she always says."

"That smells so much better than the sauce my mom makes, straight from the jar, on the rare night she serves spaghetti. My mom makes dishes like shepherd's pie."

47

Isabelle scrunches up her nose. "What's that?"

"Shepherd's pie sounds like a dessert, but it's not. Ground beef is slopped together with peas, corn, and gravy, buried under a mashed potato blanket. Nothing like a pie."

Isabelle's house is squeaky clean and a bit haunted house-ish. The chandeliers glow dim. The gold brocade draperies are closed. Soft velvet cushions cover her couch and ornate statues guard the corners. Perfect for a ghost story. Her tidy home with deep cherry wood furniture smells of lemon.

Usually her mom stays home and cooks or rests on the couch watching soap operas unless she's out shopping. Her dad works late, and Joey is at football practice. Isabelle and I rattle her house when we walk through the doors.

We head straight to the TV in the den. Isabelle introduced me to Asteroids, now my favorite video game, and I'm hooked. I love sending my mind into outer space to destroy incoming meteors as if I could save the world. Sometimes, like today, Isabelle tries to bribe me to stop playing. "I'll make you a vanilla milkshake if you shut off the game."

I give in for ice cream.

While slurping the last of the shake, Isabelle surprises me with a question. "What will you do when Randi gets out of the hospital? Will you hang out with her or me?"

The truth pops out of my mouth before I can stop it. "I'll have to see her sometimes."

Isabelle frowns, so I back pedal. "Maybe I can see her every other day—go back and forth playing with both of you. Unless you want to come with me to her house."

"I don't like Randi. I mean, not that I don't like her. It's just she's strange, and I wouldn't want to hang out with her. You have to make a choice between us." Isabelle turns her back to me. *Is she crying?*

What I want to say is: *You don't even know her. She's not weird. She's nicer than you!* But the words stay locked in my mind.

I still have a couple of weeks before I have to deal with the problem of choosing friends. How will I tell Isabelle that I want to see Randi because she is still my best friend? I don't want Isabelle to hate me either. Being in the middle is the worst.

On Mondays, Isabelle stays after school for band practice, so I choose a bus seat in the first row, next to Kimmy, a girl in Randi's class.

Before the bus even starts to move, Kimmy starts talking, barely takes a breath, and I regret my seat choice. Kimmy is like a fly buzzing in my ear. I have a strong urge to swat her.

"Have you seen Randi in the hospital yet? Our class decorated a giant card for her. Do you know how she's doing?"

"I went to visit her a month ago." For the first time, Kimmy is quiet. "She looked terrible. She had no hair and looked so skinny since she's been losing weight. And can you believe she only weighs forty pounds now?" I add, hoping to shock her with my news.

"That's not so skinny," Kimmy retorts. "I weigh forty pounds too."

Her comment irritates me, and I'm glad she gets off at the next stop. Why did I answer Kimmy and gossip about Randi like I was handing out the latest newspaper for anyone to read? What if Michael had heard us? I would've felt horrible. Good thing his mom picked him up today.

I kick the door open and drop my backpack on the floor.

"You okay? Come help me bake a cake," Mom calls from the kitchen. "And you can lick the beaters."

"What's the cake for?"

"Oh, I just felt like cooking something sweet for my sweetie."

I try not to cringe.

"How was school today?"

"Okay, I guess. I got a 93 on my math test." That's all I tell her.

"That's wonderful, honey. I'm so proud of you."

She wouldn't be so proud if she knew how I gossiped about Randi today. I wonder if Randi has a hidden side. The only flaw I can see in Randi is the one she can't help.

As we sit down for dinner, Mom can't contain her secret any longer. "Guess what I heard this afternoon?" She doesn't wait for us to guess. "Randi's coming home tomorrow, just in time for her birthday. You girls are invited to her party on Saturday. Mrs. Picconi said it will be a casual party, just family and her closest friends over for deli sandwiches and cake. That gives us two days to find a special gift."

"Wow, that's great!"

I should be excited. And I am … I think. But now I have to decide: how can I be loyal to my old friend and keep my new friend? Someone's going to be mad at me—I'm sure.

Randi has been in the hospital for two months, and I'm used to life without her. That sounds cruel, but it happened. Tomorrow, she comes home. How do I rewind my life and go back to the way it was?

9

I don't like April weather. It's too confusing. Cloudy, sunny, breezy, rainy, warm in the sunshine, cool in the shade, hot wearing long sleeves, cold wearing short sleeves. The breeze gives me goose bumps when I take off my sweater. When I put it back on, I sweat. Just as the weather can't seem to make up its mind, I'm having trouble deciding what to wear today. If I wear a dress to Randi's party, I might be chilly or overdressed. But my pants are all ugly, old, or ripped. What about color and comfort? White might get stained. Some shirts have scratchy tags. Whatever I choose—I'm not ready for today.

"What time is it?" I wait for Dad to lift his face from the Agatha Christie mystery novel.

"Well, let's see. It's five minutes later than the time I just told you. It's 1:30." He rests his book on the corner of the oak coffee table that Laurie decorated with red marker scribbles at age two. "Why don't you sign the card and we'll go over to the party in about twenty minutes. It will come sooner if you stop watching the clock or stop making me watch the clock." Dad returns to his book and I return to clock watching and tracing the red lines with my finger.

I haven't been in Randi's house for two months—since the day before her operation. Now things are different, more than just her looks. I doubt she knows I've been playing with Isabelle almost every day while she was in the hospital, unless her mother noticed and told her. This is the first time I'm keeping a secret from Randi. I'm not about to mention Isabelle today, her first week back. I'll just keep my mouth shut.

Michael greets us at the door, blowing a party horn, and wearing a pointy, red party hat. Pink and purple streamers drape across corners. Matching balloons dance around every room. In addition to the Happy Birthday sign is a Welcome Home sign hanging at the entrance to the kitchen. Billy Joel songs fill Randi's house with a familiar sound. *Is everything going to be back to normal soon? Can we play together like we used to? Am I still her best friend? Is she still my best friend?* I look around for Randi, clutching her present to my chest.

Mrs. Picconi takes Mom's hand. "I'm so glad you came. It means a lot to Randi."

I hope Mom doesn't say something to make Mrs. Picconi cry. *Remember, it's supposed to be a party.*

"We're just thrilled that Randi's home. Francie has been counting the days."

Yes, I guess I have. But not for the reason Mom thinks.

"Come in. Help yourselves to sandwiches in the kitchen. You remember my parents and my brother Joe and his wife, Barbara." As I'm peering into the other room, Mrs. Picconi puts her arm around my shoulders. "Randi will be down soon. She's feeling nauseous today." Then she calls Michael over. "I'd like you to hand out the hats and horns to all the kids and have everyone wait at the bottom of the stairs. As soon as you see Randi, blow the horns and scream happy birthday."

This is not a typical birthday party. The birthday girl is upstairs throwing up, and more adults are here than kids. Mrs. Picconi is dashing around like a wedding caterer, trying to make everything perfect.

Laurie and I stand next to Randi's cousins, Samantha and Tommy, waiting for what seems too long. Will we play games today? In past years, Randi had amazing parties with lots of kids. We made jewelry or decorated cupcakes. Her best party was like the Olympics. We ran relays, had potato sack races, and got messy in a whipped-cream pie-eating contest. I twirl the ribbon on her present and hope the party gets better when Randi comes downstairs.

I feel like an idiot just standing around, not knowing what to say. I smile at Samantha and Tommy, hoping someone will talk, because I can't think of anything worth saying. The silence lingers. Thankfully, Laurie has something to say.

"Last night Francie snored so loud, I could hear her right through the wall!"

They both laugh like it's the funniest thing they've ever heard.

Thank you, Laurie, for broadcasting this fascinating news—loud enough for every guest to hear. I want to hide my red face behind the present I'm still holding and escape all the eyes looking at me. Instead, I remember a story to tell.

"Did you hear about the time Laurie found a new use for raisins?"

Tommy shakes his head.

"Once when Laurie was potty training, Mom gave her a box of raisins to keep her on the seat. Then the phone rang. By the time Mom finished her phone call, Laurie had stuffed every raisin up her nose. She had to blow them out!"

Tommy and Samantha are laughing at Laurie now.

Laurie bulges her eyes and sticks her tongue out at me. I just smile, and enjoy her reaction. Before we can continue our humiliation battle, Randi comes down the stairs. She's wearing a red top under a cute denim jumper that hangs straight against her bony arms. Her head is covered with a matching white and red flowered scarf. Her face is pale. Her body looks thin and fragile, like the photos of concentration camp prisoners I have in my history textbook.

I almost forget to blow the party horn and cheer. Laurie nudges me and I shout "Happy birthday" with the rest of the kids. "You l-look nice," I say to Randi. "Here's your present. I hope you like it." With my eyes fixed on the ribbon instead of her scarf, I hand her the gift.

"Thanks, Francie. Sorry it took me so long to come down. I got sick again. I didn't want to come down looking like this. In the hospital, I didn't have a mirror to see how awful I look."

Smash! We turn to see a burlap bag spill clattering coins at the bottom of the stairs. Suddenly, Mr. Picconi slides down the railing and lands with a thud. He's wearing a patch over his eye, a bandana on his head, and one hand has a hook at the end. "Argh! Who here wants to have a treasure hunt?"

"Me! Me!" All the kids cheer except Randi. We search the house, trying to find the hidden, plastic gold coins, hoping to find the most and get a prize. After combing all the hiding spots, and with some helpful hinting from the grownups, Laurie finds the most. She wins a new doll. I'm not jealous since I don't play with dolls. My one doll, a costume doll from Germany and gift from Aunt Claire, looks like she was blown out the back of an airplane. She's just barely surviving in the bottom of my sister's toy box.

Randi sits alone, not participating, not eating, just watching everyone run around. I plop down next to her and swallow the last bite of a tuna sandwich.

"It must be nice to be home and sleep in your own bed again. I'm glad you're back."

"Michael told me he saw you playing with Isabelle a lot. Is she your best friend now?" Randi looks directly into my eyes, waiting for my answer.

"No. Of course not. I played with her because I had nothing else to do. You're my best friend—always. I promise I won't play with Isabelle unless you can't. Cross my heart."

"You're my only friend now, Francie. I don't want to play with anyone else, and no one else wants to play with me. I think my friends at school are afraid to see me. None of them came to visit me in the hospital and—"

Singing in the next room interrupts our conversation and we scurry over to the table.

"Happy birthday to you …" the guests attempt to sing in key. As Randi leans over to blow out the candles and make a wish, I wonder if everyone is like me, wishing her wish will come true. She must be wishing to be healthy again. As the flame disappears, I imagine her blowing all the cancer away. *Please God, let her wish come true.*

The party ends after we eat Randi's favorite white cake with raspberry filling and chocolate icing. Randi couldn't enjoy it. This wasn't her best party, but she seemed relieved to know she still has a best friend. I can't abandon her now.

Mom and Dad's voices shrink into whispers behind their bedroom door.

"Did you notice it too?" I hear Mom ask.

Don't they know that at the sound of hushed voices I put on my elephant ears?

"Poor Sal. I thought he had quit before they had kids. This is the second time we've seen him intoxicated."

Dad's voice is a smidge louder. "I feel sorry for Rita. She looked embarrassed every time he opened his mouth to speak. I'm surprised he'd —"

By accident I push the door with my head. It creaks.

"Francie, is that you?"

"Yah. I just wanted to tell you *The Love Boat* is on." *That was a close one.*

"Okay. We'll be out in a minute."

In that minute, I open a dictionary. I-n-t-o-x …

10

One week later, Mrs. Picconi is at our front door. "Randi would like Francie to come to the city with us tomorrow morning for her radiation treatment. Could she be ready at nine o'clock?"

Mom doesn't answer right away. I hope she's thinking of a way to say no. "Sure. I'll have her ready and give her some money for lunch."

What? Is she kidding? No way. I gave up hospitals after the last visit.

"Great! Randi will feel less miserable if Francie is with her."

I guess I don't have a say in this. Going to the hospital once was enough for me. This time will be worse. I have no idea what radiation is, but it reminds me of Frankenstein getting zapped to life.

All night I toss and turn, in and out of nightmares, waiting for morning. When the sun rises, I'm tired. But before I can catch my breath and wake up, their car honks. I almost choke on a Rice Krispy that goes down the wrong pipe as I leave the half-eaten bowl of cereal on the table and race out the door.

Randi wiggles over on the back seat, and I slide in next to her. "I'm so glad you're coming with us. I hate going there. I have to lie completely still. When it's over, I throw up. I feel weak—even the next day. It's horrible." Randi leans her head back and closes her eyes. I do the same and imagine it was my appointment. It would be worse to go through this without a friend.

I can't look at Randi without seeing the C word. How can I have fun with my best friend when I don't understand what's happening to her? And do I really want to understand? I'd rather play kickball with her like we used to before radiation appointments. *God, can you heal her tumor so she's not sick anymore, and I can have my life back?*

In the car, we try to come up with enough games to occupy ourselves for the two-hour trip. I give the first clue. "I'm thinking of an animal that lives in water and also walks on land."

Randi guesses. "Is it a frog?"

"No. Too small."

"Is it a whale?"

"Whales can't walk on land. Imagine a killer whale with legs."

Mrs. Picconi joins in. "I'd never go to the beach again." We all laugh.

Before she can guess alligator, we arrive at the hospital. I follow Randi's steps down the corridor to the elevator. She leads the way and points to a framed poster of Claude Monet's *White Water Lilies*. "We turn right at the pond painting." Randi pinches her nose. "You better hold yours too. Smells like fish sandwiches today … for the ones who can eat."

"We go up to the ninth floor." The elevator doors open to a sparkling clean lobby, and I follow Randi again into a world I've never seen. We pass by a child crying in her mother's arms. I can't believe this is Randi's world.

The waiting area is decorated in bright yellow, orange, and purple. The happy colors clash. I think of children soldiers who fight enemies inside their own bodies. *Why do kids have to fight this battle?* I see relief ripple across faces when the nurse calls someone else's name to the front line. *Will the radiation weapons work?*

I sit down next to a little boy, about five years old, with thinning hair. He colors a picture of Superman and carefully outlines the cape. I wonder if he imagines flying away to save people.

A teenage girl in a Gap t-shirt holds a baseball cap and stares at a girl who is the color of a corpse. Will she need that cap when she leaves? Will she be a survivor or one of the casualties of war? Watching kids suffer bothers me more than I thought it would.

Randi slumps in her chair and traces the flowers on her sleeve. I wonder which group she belongs to.

A young nurse with curly black hair and a gentle smile handles the roll call. Her glasses slide down her nose as she checks each name off a clipboard. "Randi Picconi, you're next. Come with me."

Randi ducks behind her mom and whispers, "I don't want to go. Don't make me do this anymore. Please?"

Mrs. Picconi leans over, adjusts Randi's scarf and looks into her eyes. "I know, but you have to do this. I want my little girl to get better. Come on, I'll be right next to you. We'll close our eyes and pretend we're birds soaring over beautiful meadows with wildflowers swaying and waterfalls splashing us."

Randi doesn't smile. "I wish I *could* fly out of here," she says.

Mrs. Picconi turns around just before they pass through the door. "Francie, we'll be back in about twenty minutes."

I nod, and she escorts Randi into the battle zone.

I read last month's *Seventeen* magazine for longer than twenty minutes and try not to stare at the other children in the waiting room. I read every single page and learn the latest hairstyles, how to apply make-up with a natural glow, and how to flirt with boys. I even try a few subtle exercises "sure to tighten your buttocks," the author claims. But when I lift my head out of the magazine and look into the faces of these sick kids, I see that none of this stuff matters. No one cares about flirting when she is throwing up. People don't care about hairstyles when they don't have hair. No one cares about having tight muscles when he is just skin and bones. I'd like to crumple the magazine and stop caring about the dumb stuff.

By the time Mrs. Picconi and Randi return, I'm half-asleep with the magazine on my feet. "Sorry, you waited so long. Randi was throwing up." Mrs. Picconi speaks for Randi who looks like she lost this battle. Her scarf is off, and Mrs. Picconi is holding a throw-up bag in front of her, just in case.

"Francie, please put Randi's scarf back on for me. My hands are full." Mrs. Picconi takes a deep breath and sighs.

I place the scarf on Randi's bare head. Up close, her skin looks smooth and transparent like a baby's. She seems so helpless. It's not a fair fight.

For the drive home, Randi sleeps in the back seat. I sit in front. Mrs. Picconi chats about the easy stuff like school and the weather, but my eyelids droop as the warm sunlight flickers in between buildings. My head clunks against the window.

"Here. Use this as a pillow." Mrs. Picconi hands me her thick, pale blue sweater, and I snuggle into it. It's much better than hard glass against my head.

When we arrive home, Mrs. Picconi carries Randi's limp body into the house to put her to bed. I wave good-bye, but neither one sees me. As I walk home, I think about what excuse I can give the next time she asks me to go with her. I never want to see that place again.

11

This week my alternating game began. On Mondays, Wednesdays, and Fridays, Randi goes to the hospital for radiation. On those days, I can play with Isabelle. On Tuesdays and Thursdays, I knock at Randi's door to find out if she is feeling well enough to play. More often than not, Randi's days get changed to Isabelle days. Saturdays are split. In the morning, I hang out with Isabelle at the ceramic shop, and in the afternoon, I see Randi. Sundays are always for Randi. I wonder how long I can stick with this friend schedule before someone gets mad or I go crazy.

I'm sure Mrs. Picconi wants me glued to Randi's side. She just called Mom and told her, "Francie needs to be ready in five minutes to come with us to the hardware store." I understand why—Randi needs a best friend—but I'm getting tired of being dragged to do what I don't want to do. So today I'll spend this sunny spring day staring at tools.

After hanging up the phone, Mom rushes me out the door, sympathizing with Mrs. Picconi. Everyone—Randi's parents, my parents, neighbors, and even her little brother who I catch spying on me every so often—wants me to be the perfect friend.

"Is your dad coming?" He could turn any errand into a game. Randi says her father in a hardware store is like a toddler in a lollipop factory.

Randi looks down at her bracelet and spins it a few times. "No. He fell asleep on the couch again." Even though no one else is in the car, she whispers. "Mom's real mad 'cause Dad said he'd go buy a new screen for the back door to replace the one he stuck his foot through. She said she's pressed for time and has to catch up on grading papers for her class. Mom doesn't like it when Dad sleeps all day. He never used to—"

Mrs. Picconi gets in and slams the car door. "Okay, we're off." She looks between Randi and me as she reverses. We don't talk. Elton John is singing, and Mrs. Picconi is mumbling to herself.

Soon after we enter the store, I realize why Mrs. Picconi wanted me to come. In public, people of all ages stare at Randi. Some try to look like they're not, but they are. Some quickly look away, and some offer an awkward smile, but whisper when she passes by. Randi ignores the stares, as if they don't bother her, but she is quieter than usual. "Can we leave now?" she asks her mom after ten minutes in the store. No one hears me arguing.

Now that summer is almost here, Randi has to stay inside, away from the bright sun. When I'm with her, I feel trapped in a cage. I want to unlock the bars and fly outside.

I can't concentrate in school either. A warm breeze blows through the open classroom window and tickles my neck. Sparrows play tag and dart through the blossoming cherry trees. The sun is calling me out, but I have to stay late for the dress rehearsal after school. Tonight is the play.

***

I race out to the car in my brown pants and green shirt, the outfit worn under my tree costume. Dad is already waiting in the car, ready to get me to the play before anyone else arrives. "Okay little tree. Here we go. Are you nervous?"

"No. Just wish the butterflies in my tummy would fly away, and I could stop my legs from shaking."

"Don't worry. I'm sure you'll be the best actress in the play. You're growing branches off your shoulders from rehearsing so much."

I keep telling myself four simple lines about snow isn't much—no way can I mess that up. Why do I keep hearing that other voice, the one that tells me: *You can't speak in front of hundreds of people? You're too shy. Nothing will come out of your mouth when you open it.*

Standing next to my tree parents on stage, I see everything through two round holes: the dim lights, full auditorium, flashing cameras, staring people, and the silence. I wait for my turn to speak, thankful I can hide behind the cardboard. Will the words come out when I open my mouth? I need to take a deep breath and speak loudly, aiming toward the back row. They need to hear me—even if I'm just a baby tree. Nothing else matters now except doing this right.

The snowflakes dance across the stage. That's my cue!

"I love snow. I just love it."

Papa tree speaks: "I hate it, just hate it. I am too many rings old to enjoy cold, heavy, clumps of snow sitting on my branches."

I open my mouth again: "Well, I'm still a kid, one hundred forty-four and a half years young. I think it tickles."

Mama tree turns her cardboard toward me, bumping father tree in the process. "I think you'd better close your eyes and get some sleep, little one, if you want to grow tall like your father. In the morning, you can watch the rabbits hop through the snow."

I take a deep breath and shout my last lines: "Look, Mama! There's a bunny hopping right now." At her cue, Nina hops by in her bunny suit. I have to stifle my laugh when she wiggles her tail. My tree probably looks like it's dancing.

Yes! I did it. I was loud, remembered my lines, and even enjoyed being on stage. I'm not sure it was worth twisting my stomach into knots, but it may be worth the celebration afterward at Friendly's for ice cream sundaes. Before that, I need to remove my branches, wipe off the green face-paint, and change back into the real me.

But I'm not sure who the real me is. I'm not the same with Randi as I am with Isabelle or Nina. And I don't know who I want to be. Sometimes I think invisible is the best choice.

Today, on the last day of the school year, I get to be silly at Nina's house. I can joke and laugh while riding on her bus. No one picks on Nina. She's the best soccer player in fifth grade, so no one bothers me, her friend. At Nina's I don't worry about who I should hang out with, Randi or Isabelle. I'm in another part of town, away from my troubles on Hartwell Drive. I wish my parents would let me escape here more often, but they don't like this area. It makes no sense to me. Last week I turned eleven—"too old for a birthday party"—but I'm still too young to ride my bike ten minutes away from my house. Do my parents own a book called *One Hundred Parenting Rules to Confuse Your Child?*

Nina rules her house from the time she gets off the bus until her mom gets home from work. I would be scared to be alone that much, but Nina tells me she doesn't mind. She controls the snack drawer, the television, and most important, the phone.

We gobble Twinkies in her den and watch soap operas. No one tells us not to. It's great.

"Let's go get everyone for a soccer game," says Nina.

"Okay, but I stink. I don't play much soccer."

"That doesn't matter. I'll teach you what my papa taught me. He coaches soccer at the high school."

"So that's why you're so good!"

"He's had me doing drills since I was two. When I see him on the weekends, we play soccer. Rain or snow, we play soccer. It's crazy fun."

The ball charges at me in defense, closer and closer until it's right in front of me. I'm ready, but the ball disappears before I'm able to stop myself. I kick nothing but air as hard as I can, causing me to trip and fall on my knee while a fourth grade boy dribbles the ball the other way. Now I'm determined to do better. I don't want to make a fool of myself again. I brush the gravel out of my scraped knee.

Why is Nina yelling at me?

"Watch—!"

I turn my head for an instant. "What?"

Whack! The muddy ball pounds my head, leaving an imprint. I drop to the ground. "Ow! That hurt." I try not to cry, but I'm practically seeing stars.

"Are you okay? I'm so sorry. Didn't you hear me yell watch out?" Nina is trying not to laugh. "Let's go get some ice."

At the table, while freezing my head off and on, Nina drops an ice cube on her toe and hollers, "Oh shneer!" The two of us burst into giggles at her silly word. "My mom sends me to my room for an hour if I curse. She doesn't want me to sound like the kids next door."

We play a game of inventing words. "Peezy-sneezy: when a person tries to hold back a sneeze and it comes out like a whistle anyway. Fernhop: when parents embarrass their child and the child wishes to turn back time and erase what they said. Poo-doo-da: dog poo on bottom of sneakers."

"Can you teach me some Spanish words?"

"*Sí*. Say *hola* for hello."

Nina's mom walks through the door. She looks more like a sister than a mother with her wavy brown hair pulled back in a ponytail. She's barely taller than Nina and wears a braided headband that seems familiar—like the one Nina wore last week.

"*Hola, mi hija*!" Mrs. Sanchez chatters in Spanish. When she notices me, her words slow down and change to difficult-to-understand English. "What a long day! I am so glad to be home. So who is thees preetty girl?"

"This is my friend, Francie. She's in my class."

"Ooh, nice to meet you." Mrs. Sanchez wraps her arms around me and kisses my cheek. She smells like laundry detergent and burgers. I love the way she rolls her *r*'s when she repeats my name. "Nina's talked about you. She told me you have a very sick friend. I put her on the prayer list at my church."

"Mmm ... I smell burgers." Nina reaches for the greasy white bag, grabs some french fries, and puts a couple in my mouth that hang out like cigarettes.

"Thanks."

"Mama, can Francie eat with us?"

"*Sí, yes.* I wish I had cooked something special, but it's takeout night."

Nina hands out paper plates, and we take our burgers to plastic TV trays in the den. "Let's eat here. There's too much mail on the kitchen table."

We chomp on fries while watching *Phil Donahue.* Today's guests are talking about their addictions.

Nina slurps her soda. "You gotta be crazy to go on this show and tell the world your problems."

I love Nina's house. My life would be much easier if my parents would let me ride my bike this far. I could hang out here and escape my friend juggling on Hartwell Drive.

I don't have many friends, so why am I caught in this triangle? An eleven-year-old shouldn't have such a complicated life. What will I do this summer when I have to choose between friends every day?

12

"No, definitely not," says Mrs. Picconi when Randi gives her Mrs. Torelli's invitation to a "beginning of summer" pool party. Randi and I plead, and she promises to wear the scarf in the water and apply tons of sun block. After ten minutes of begging, Mrs. Picconi gives in and says, "Okay, but only if you keep your head dry."

Randi gives me a high five. I'm surprised Mrs. Picconi said yes. She probably wants Randi to be included—to have some *normal* fun. I'm glad Randi can come to the party, but how can she have fun in a pool without getting wet?

Before we jump in, Mrs. Picconi gathers the kids. "Please promise you won't splash. Randi has to keep her scarf dry and her head protected from the sun."

"We promise." Randi stands next to her mom and rolls her eyes as she speaks.

In keeping our promise, we all use the steps to get in the pool instead of jumping off the side. We play a round of Marco Polo. I peek so I don't touch Randi with my wet hands. The pool stays calm for a while until one person forgets.

"Five, four, three, two, one, watch out!" shouts Isabelle, landing a cannonball off the diving board. This leads to a splashing battle. Water in my eyes, down my throat, drenching my face as I shovel it back in their faces. Everyone's wet. As I hop on one foot to shake water out of my right ear, someone shrieks.

"*What* are you doing? I told you Randi can't get her head wet!" Mrs. Picconi yells at Isabelle.

Everyone freezes in place and stares at Mrs. Picconi. Randi looks away. We all *did* promise not to splash, but didn't know that Mrs. Picconi would flip out if we broke our promise and had some fun.

Mrs. Picconi waves a firm hand to call us out. "Randi, Michael, Francie … please get out of the pool right now." We file out, leaving a trail of wet footprints. "It's time to leave. Randi, you need to change into dry clothes. Francie, see you for dinner in thirty minutes." Mrs. Picconi wraps Randi tightly in a Disneyland towel and rushes her toward the backyard gate. She leaves her glass of lemonade, half empty, on the table.

Pleading with my eyes, I stare at Mom, hoping she will say something to correct Mrs. Picconi before she leaves. Can't she tell her that I'm allowed to stay in the pool—that I can stay in until my lips turn blue? Why can't I do what I want? I wish I hadn't agreed to eat over there tonight. They eat dinner so early. I practically just had lunch.

Mom gives me a look that says it all. I should understand how hard it is for Randi. She must hate watching kids play and do things without her. I should go with them. It's the right thing to do so I push all the grumbling down to my toes.

I grab my towel and shake my head to Isabelle with a quick "sorry-I-can't-help-it" look. Isabelle turns away. She must be mad that Randi came to the pool party and ruined it. Isabelle's sweet face disappears just as an angry cloud hides the sun. Seeing her frown makes me think. We blame Randi for ending our fun, but it's not her fault. It's not her mom's fault either for wanting to protect Randi.

Under the grey sky, I shiver as I walk home.

On my way over to Randi's, my stomach growls; swimming got me hungry again. Carnival music sings in the street as the ice-cream truck turns the corner onto Hartwell Drive. As I knock on Randi's door, Isabelle charges across her lawn to go to the ice-cream man before the truck disappears. I wave to her, but maybe she didn't see me. I wish I had fifty cents in my pocket.

I thought I heard someone shout to come in so I do. Mrs. Picconi is shouting, but not to me.

"You have to get upstairs—now! The kids are about to have dinner, and you're lying here in your pajamas, a mess."

I shrink back to the door, unsure of what to do.

Mr. Picconi trips in front of me. He heads upstairs and says, "Sorry. Go on in."

He does look a mess—like he just rolled out of bed after a night of bad dreams.

From the hallway, I hear the sound of bottles clinking together. Mrs. Picconi storms past me holding a black trash bag.

"Hi, Francie. Randi's in the kitchen," she says through tight lips.

The next sound I hear is glass smashing in the metal garbage can outside and muffled sobs.

Randi is setting the table. "We're having burgers, macaroni, and salad for dinner." She doesn't mention the scene that just happened. She folds a napkin, careful to match the corners. A tear drops and ruins it, so she crumples the napkin into a ball, wipes her eyes and starts over. *Is this a typical night at the Picconi's now?*

I reach for some napkins to help. "It smells good. I'm starved after swimming." *That was stupid. Why did I have to bring up the pool?*

"I'm sorry you had to get out of the pool so soon. I didn't want to ruin the party."

"You didn't ruin anything. I wanted to get out anyway." *Well, if this was true, I wouldn't feel like I just won the worst friend award.*

It feels strange to eat dinner here, not because it's Randi's house, but because I'm used to my usual chair and not worrying about manners. Did I talk with my mouth full? Did anyone notice that I dropped a piece of lettuce on the floor? Should I pick it up or pretend I didn't notice it drop?

Mr. Picconi's seat is still empty as I bite a corner of the burger. Something feels wrong as we eat without him here joking. "This burger is delicious with lettuce and tomato on it." That's all I can think of saying.

"I'm glad you like it." Mrs. Picconi passes me some more salad. "Tomatoes are good for you. When you kids are finished, you can have some pudding for dessert."

Pudding is okay, but not as good as Twinkies at Nina's or milkshakes at Isabelle's. I think pudding must remind Randi of hospital food. She doesn't look too excited about dessert either.

We take turns describing our favorite dishes. I imagine filling Mr. Picconi's empty seat with stacks of casseroles and pies. After speaking a few times, and realizing no one is angry at me for my friendship with Isabelle, I start to feel one-inch better. Maybe they're not watching every move I make and judging everything I say.

Pleased with myself for passing the table manners test, I step out of the Picconi's house. Ahh … fresh air! I can catch fireflies, cartwheel all the way home, and tumble at gymnastics class with Isabelle tomorrow. And no homework for two months! The crickets' chirping sounds like party horns to me. I bend down to pick up a dandelion and blow my wish into the warm air. I wish for more of this freedom.

13

I wish Isabelle's mom didn't blast her horn like a fire engine and draw attention to their Cadillac. As I run to the car, I notice Michael playing ball, watching us drive away. If he squeals to Randi, I'll have to tell her about where I went. Nothing is simple. Gymnastics has always been Randi's favorite sport. After four years of gymnastics classes, her back and legs could stretch like rubber-bands, and she was fearless on the beam. Mr. Picconi even set up a practice beam in their back yard. She loved gymnastics until her head hurt too much to turn upside down.

I try to forget about Randi missing gymnastics and enjoy the ride on the slippery leather seats in Isabelle's fancy car.

The tiny room where we practice stinks of dirty socks and powder. The teacher, Mrs. Korn, is tiny too—not the size of someone who can spot me for a back-handspring and keep my head off the ground. Her daughter, the best student in the class, looks like a younger clone of her mom with longer hair. She does backbends like she's made of rubber, like Randi.

I'm like cardboard. I can bend, but kind of awkward and stiff, not exactly the look of a gymnast. Most of the girls are younger than eleven and have trained for a few years already. My body doesn't like these unnatural positions. Mrs. Korn keeps telling me to straighten my leg when I cartwheel, but it bends every time, afraid of leaving solid ground.

I need to find a place where Isabelle and I can practice without Randi seeing us. If we get too close to her yard, she could see us from her window. I don't want to exclude Randi, but who knows how long it'll be before she can do gymnastics again? When will she do what she used to, anyway? Wasn't that operation supposed to make her better?

"Francie. Yes or no? Did you hear me?" whispers Isabelle.

We're in line to practice front walkovers. I shrug my shoulders. "Sorry, uh, did you ask me to go see your poodle?" From the look on Isabelle's face, that's *way* off. Sometimes I'd swear I live in a bubble.

Isabelle wags her head back and forth. "I asked you if you want to go in my pool when we get home. I don't have a poodle! You know my mom would never let a "smelly animal" into our house. She thinks a gerbil is too hairy."

Zoned out again. "I'd love to go in the pool. Forget I said poodle."

"Girls, be quiet and pay attention. You're distracting the others who want to learn."

Now I've got the giggles. Isabelle catches my disease. Angry at our disrespect, Mrs. Korn tells us to sit down against the mirror until we are ready to join the class properly.

I want another turn before the class ends, so I stop laughing and put on my sorry and humble face. With no one to laugh at, Isabelle is quiet too. We apologize and tiptoe to the back of the line.

In Isabelle's pool, later that afternoon, we become Olympic gymnasts doing front flips, back flips, handstand contests, somersaults under water, and backward dives off the diving board. I never worry even once if we're being too loud or if Randi can hear us two houses away. Not until I run home on bare toes and drip past Randi's house do I think of her. At the same time, I hear a nursery rhyme in my head, one Dad always read to me:

There was a little girl
Who had a little curl
Right in the middle of her forehead;
And when she was good,
She was very, very good.
But when she was bad, she was horrid!

Did Dad read that rhyme with the hope that I would be the girl *without* the curl, who *always* shared her toys, and *always* listened to her parents, and *always* cared about others more than herself? I'm not that girl. Sometimes I have the curl. I tire of doing the right thing. I hear the sounds of splashing and want to dive into the pool. My curl springs back to my forehead, and I think *stop caring. Get me out of here!*

***

"Do you want to play air hockey?" Randi looks out the window. "I know it's not as much fun as gymnastics, but at least it's something."

"Sure. It's been a while since I played. Bet you five cents that I'll win. I'd bet more if there was more in my pocket." Did she see me doing gymnastics on the lawn with Isabelle? Unless she asks, I won't tell.

"Okay, five cents to the winner." Randi whacks at the puck. Her eyes say, "I can win."

I play just as hard, forgetting that I want her to win. The orange circle hypnotizes me, bouncing back and forth, back and forth. Each time it collides with plastic, the vibration tickles my hand. Randi wins by one point.

"I won! Where's my nickel?" Randi asks, holding back a proud smirk.

She must be getting better. Before her operation, this game would have been way too noisy, like a hammer hitting her brain. But now she doesn't complain about the noise at all. Maybe she just needs to have a goal for beating cancer. Will she try as hard as she did in air hockey to beat her disease?

I bow to Randi and place the reward in her hands. "Here's your nickel. That was a close game. Want to play again?"

"Nah, I want to sit outside and have some iced tea in the shade."

I like that idea. Finally, some sun.

After we have our drink and play some guessing games, Randi dozes off on the lounge chair. Her scarf is crooked. I'm left sitting in silence, wondering what I should do, until a voice startles me.

"She's wiped out from the radiation yesterday." Mrs. Picconi takes a deep breath and straightens Randi's scarf without waking her. "She was trying her hardest to stay awake and be more entertaining so you'd want to come here more often."

"I'd like to come here more," I lie, trying to explain and apologize at the same time. "I'm sorry...but sometimes Isabelle asks me to go over to her house."

"I know. It's just that you were Randi's best friend. Now, you're her only friend. And she feels excluded. She spends so much time alone, crying. I hate seeing her this way." Mrs. Picconi gathers the empty glasses with one hand and wipes the sweat off Randi's forehead with a napkin. "You're a nice girl, Francie. I know you don't mean to hurt Randi. That's why I wanted to have this talk. Well, you should probably go home now. She won't be waking up for a while."

"Okay. Tell Randi I said good-bye … and I'll see her tomorrow." Once again, a lump swells in my throat. There is no way I can play with Isabelle for a few days. I run home to hide my tears and my guilt.

I take the short cut, dashing between the bushes and leaping over the jagged root protruding out of the ground, but not high enough. I trip and land in the flowerbed. Blood drips from my scraped up knees and tears pour out in sobs for the pain I felt before I fell. Now I have an excuse to cry.

I am an eleven-year-old with a hard job—being Randi's friend, responsible for her happiness. Isn't that God's job? Didn't He let her get this disease? Why does it all fall on me? Even if I try my hardest, I'll never be able to please everyone. Randi needs me, but sometimes I just want to give up trying, and do what I want. Could I close the picture album of our fun memories and never look at it again? Never think about Randi. Never think about hurting her. Never think about her sad eyes watching me from her window.

Could I do that?

14

I wish someone had invented a way to be in two places at once. Then Isabelle wouldn't be pouting and standing with her hands on her hips.

"We were supposed to work on our show yesterday," she complains.

"I know, but Mrs. Picconi made me feel guilty for not seeing Randi enough."

"You don't see me enough either. We had plans to work on the show and go swimming."

"But I'm her only friend. I have to see her sometimes, even if I'd rather be here with you." Although right now, I'm not so sure.

"Whatever … let's just practice. We don't have much time left."

"Okay." Giving Isabelle a challenging look, I shout, "Race you to my house," and dash down her hill at my top speed.

Isabelle charges after me. "Wait up! You didn't say go."

She still beats me there. I must be part tortoise.

The race helps us forget our squabble and get excited again about our idea to perform a gymnastics show and sell tickets to kids in the neighborhood. For an hour, we glue ourselves to the television, recording commercials with lively songs onto her tape recorder. We take our music outside and make up routines.

I just wish the show could be somewhere else, somewhere hidden from Randi. The problem: my front lawn is the best area with the most flat space. Isabelle's lawn would be out of sight, but has a slope to it. It's good for sledding but not tumbling. A humungous rock sits at the slope's end. If one of us flipped into it, our show would end in an ambulance. Of course, performing on my front yard will give Randi a balcony view.

I should tell Randi about the show. I know it, but don't think I can. After we clear my yard of sticks and pebbles, we blast the tape of fuzzy-sounding soda songs: "I drink Dr. Pepper, don't ya know …" and attempt to choreograph some routines.

"You could do a front handspring running this way, and I'll do the same thing from over there—like a crisscross." Isabelle tries out her idea.

"I like that. How 'bout we turn at the same time and do two front walkovers next to each other?"

We take turns demonstrating what we imagine to see if it works. When it does, we hurry to write it down to remember the routine. The sun beats down, cooking us, as we continue this pattern all afternoon—her suggestions and mine, back and forth, trial and error—until we are hot and sunburned and know all the commercials by heart.

The words repeat in my mind. *Just one calorie.* Isabelle and I hop around like rabbits in our own creative world. Tumbling, singing, and laughing, we collapse from heat and exhaustion in the shade. Since we're already in our bathing suits, it seems a perfect time to dive into Isabelle's pool.

Mrs. Picconi gets out of her car just as Isabelle and I run down the street in our bare feet and bathing suits. She says hi. We say hi back, and I'm not so happy anymore. Why can't I ignore the Picconis and erase this ever-present, stomach-twisting guilt?

Heading home from Isabelle's pool, I push my wet hair back and notice a pea-size bump on my head, behind my left ear. *What the heck is that?* On the slight chance I might grow a second head and transform into a strange alien, I decide to show Mom.

Showing Mom was a mistake. Her face turns pale as if she did see an alien. She rummages through the cabinets until she finds a match. "You have a tick!"

"How would I get a tick?"

"Probably from doing headstands on the grass."

"What's the match for?"

"I'm going to burn it out."

"No way! You're gonna light my hair on fire."

"Okay, forget it. Come on … let's go." She rushes me into the car, acting as if I am about to die. At the same time, Dad arrives home from work.

Dad leans out the car window. "Where are you going, Fran?"

"I'm taking Francie to the hospital. She has a tick on her head." Mom drives off in a hurry before Dad can say a word. He looks bewildered as I wave to him out the back window.

Across from me in the emergency room waiting area, a man with two black eyes holds an icepack on his nose. He explains to me—though I didn't ask—that his wife broke his nose during a golfing lesson. "I was surprised all right, when she swung that club and let go. I've never seen so many stars in the daylight."

Then his wife blurts out: "Honey, you shouldn't stand so close when I'm swinging a club."

"You're right, dear. I should've waited on the next hill."

On the other side of the room, a grey-haired lady sits with her bare foot raised on a chair. The whole foot is swollen and purple. I hope this doesn't happen to me when I reach old age. I could never put toenail polish on a foot that looked like that!

Nothing looks wrong with me other than the worried expression plastered on my face. I keep telling myself I'm fine, healthy as can be, as long as I don't touch the bump, the swollen insect sucking my blood. Yuck! If I think about it, I might throw up.

I hear my name. A nurse calls us to the front desk to fill out some papers. She asks me why I'm there. I whisper, "I think I have a tick behind my ear."

"What?" she screams. This nurse must be deaf or stupid.

I glance around to see if the other patients are listening, and answer in a louder whisper. "I have a tick." Some eavesdroppers giggle from across the room. When the questions are finished, I sit down again and slouch behind an outdated Health magazine.

Ten minutes later the nurse calls me over again. "Francie McLean, go in the first room on the right. The doctor will be in soon to remove the tick."

Whoa! She said that super loud! Everyone on the first floor could hear that. I'll bet the other patients sitting in the lobby, who have been waiting for three hours, are wondering why I went first over a broken nose and elephant feet. Only Mom would think a tick is more urgent. I rush to the first room on the right to hide my red face.

"Hello, I'm here for the emergency operation." The doctor bends down to avoid bumping his head in the doorway and shakes my hand. His wild, curly black hair frames his oval face. He reminds me of those pencils with goofy-eyes and hair that you can shake. "You must be the young patient suffering from insectivitis. This is extremely serious. We *must* operate now."

Does this doctor honestly think humiliating me is going to make me laugh? It's a good thing he's a doctor and not a comedian! *Just get it over with already* is what I'd like to yell at him. But I go along with his stupid joke and smile.

"Imagine you're sitting on an iceberg in Alaska. Your ear will feel cold for a few seconds, and *voila,* the beastie will be out." Doctor Goofy's explanation takes longer than the actual procedure. "Here's the little critter you were hosting." He shows me the swollen tick, which I did not want to see. Thanks, Doc. I bet he can't wait to share this story for a good laugh. He might tell every doctor he knows, spreading the news until it reaches the west coast.

At least the tick is out, and Mom is calm again—unlike Dad who is anything but calm when we get home. He had ticks on him every summer day as a kid playing in tall reeds along the beach in Montauk. How could he possibly understand the panic Mom felt? I guess she has a fear of bugs or hates seeing anything bad happen to me.

"I can't believe you took her to the hospital for a tick! You know how much this will cost since you didn't call her primary doctor first?" Dad rants for a while, so I leave the room. I can't blame him. I wish we didn't go to the hospital. I hate going there, especially for such a stupid reason. My stupid bug-bump removal seems ridiculous compared to the difficult removal of Randi's tumor. At least now I can say I've been to the hospital for something. Then again ... maybe I'll pretend this never happened.

The next day is an ordinary summer Saturday. Dad waters the flowers. Laurie roller-skates on the driveway. I practice handstands alone since Isabelle is at her cousin's birthday party. Randi's napping, and Nina is at her father's house for the weekend. Mom strolls down the driveway to talk with Mr. and Mrs. Picconi as they stop their bikes by our house. The Picconis usually go for a walk or bike ride around the block each evening before the sun sets. This time I can't tell if Mrs. Picconi is laughing or crying.

Laurie and I hide by the car to listen. "We thought she was improving, but today we found out ..." Mrs. Picconi's voice fades into the air. "Randi has another tumor growing in a different part of her brain." She covers her mouth and doubles over in bursts of sobs.

"Oh, Rita, that's awful!" Mom says. I look over the bumper to witness the horrific scene. Mom leans over the bike and hugs Mrs. Picconi, more like supports her from fainting. Mr. Picconi wipes his eyes and whimpers. Dad shakes his head, looking distraught. I hurry back to the house so no one hears me crying.

I can't believe they have to relive the nightmare. Will Randi have to repeat everything she went through: more surgery, more radiation, more hospital, and more grief? I can't believe this is happening. My faith in doctors, in God, and in life is at an all-time low. *When will this end?*

15

"The night-blooming cereus is one of the strangest flowers God created." The botanist on channel 13 points to the amazing flower, and I stop flipping channels. "This white star-like flower has an extravagant fragrance, but can hardly be enjoyed. Rarely seen, this desert flower in the cactus family blooms on one midsummer's night for a few hours— then shrivels and dies, never to be seen again." I turn the TV off in disgust. I was hoping to be distracted, but even a nature show reminds me of Randi. I can't understand why God would destroy Randi's perfect life. Why would God bother creating a beautiful girl if he knew he was just going to take back her beauty? *What's the point?*

I sink into the couch and stare at the black, empty screen on the television. I'm not thinking about anything, not feeling anything. The air around me is holding me down, paralyzing me.

Is this real? No one told me that cancer could return. After all the effort it took to get rid of the first tumor, it's hopeless if the cancer can just start growing in a new spot, like weeds that take over a flower garden. I wish Dr. Googly eyes could freeze it away like he did the tick.

All those stupid feelings are rising again like a heated thermometer. I worry for Randi. I worry for myself. *Will my life ever be normal?*

Dad sits down next to me. "I guess you overheard our conversation with Mr. and Mrs. Picconi."

I nod and swipe away a tear.

"It's horrible. We *all* thought she was recovering."

We both stare into the blank television screen. Emotions hang in the air, thick, like smoke, without words. He rests his arm on my shoulders. The silence is painful. Dad must feel it too. He turns on the TV.

After watching an episode of *Little House on the Prairie* and feeling sad about Laura's older sister, Mary, going blind, I decide to go to bed. Too many problems for one night.

My dad kisses my forehead. "It would be nice if you could go see Randi sometime tomorrow and cheer her up."

Pressure. More pressure to do the right thing. Why didn't he suggest I go see a movie with Isabelle, have fun, relax. Do I have to be perfect? I just can't bear another miserable Randi day.

Instead of pleasing Dad, I'm going to do what I want. I want to see Isabelle and prepare for our show. What could I say to Randi anyway? Isabelle and I have to make the posters and hang them, or no one will come to the show we've been rehearsing for. We can't wait another day.

Almost every Isabelle day, we have practiced until the fireflies twinkled. The show has to be this Friday, since school starts next week. At night, I can hardly sleep; the songs play in my head and I imagine the gymnastics routine, again and again.

Even though Dad wanted me to visit Randi today, I'm determined to walk down the street with my eyes focused straight ahead. I won't even look at Randi's house. I'm definitely not going there today.

Just before I pass Randi's driveway, Mrs. Picconi happens to be coming out the door. My plan is not working. Now I definitely *am* going to end up in Randi's house.

"Hi, Francie. Go on in. Randi's awake," calls Mrs. Picconi. She smiles and holds the door for me. "She'll be happy to see you."

Just great.

I change my direction and head inside. Now I'm stuck here, and Isabelle will be mad that I didn't show up. Maybe I can think of an excuse—not a lie—to leave early and sneak over to Isabelle's without telling Randi where I'm going.

Randi is sitting at the kitchen table and threading bead necklaces, something I would enjoy doing if I weren't set on rehearsing for the show. "Hi, Randi. I can't stay too long," I pick up a green bead and gaze through it. "My mom wants me to clean my room."

She always wants me to clean, so it's a half-truth.

"That's okay. You can make at least one necklace before you go." Randi hands me the bowl swirling with colorful beads.

It would be easier to leave if she were grumpy, if she took her anger out on me. I mean, she must be upset about the news, but she isn't showing it. Instead, she seems glad I'm here. I sit still for an hour and thread beads, which is hard to do while staring at the strawberry shaped clock on the wall.

The beads slip out of my hands, one after the other. They clink on the ceramic tiles. Randi is concentrating on her necklace. I am concentrating on finding a reason to leave. I can hear her breathing slow and steady. I wish Randi would say something.

Another half hour passes. I'm itching to be outside. "I better go now or my mom will be mad."

"Maybe you can come over when you're done cleaning."

"Maybe, if she doesn't have any other chores for me to do." I tie the necklace around my neck.

"Ooh, I love it! Now you look too fancy to clean!"

"Thanks. Too bad my mom won't care how fancy I look. She'll just hand me the broom."

After saying good-bye, I race over to Isabelle's to explain what took me so long, praying Randi won't find out that I didn't go home to clean. I should feel guilty, but I'm too excited, and I have other chores:

Monday: make and hang the posters.

Tuesday: practice; gather costumes together.

Wednesday: practice. Practice. Practice.

Thursday: practice; get refreshments ready.

Saturday: perform our star-studded debut!

After a lot of arguing, Isabelle and I decide that *The Shining Stars* would be the best title for our show. We trace star stencils and pour glitter all over bright posters advertising the best performance ever on Hartwell Drive. I'm careful to hang them away from Randi and Michael's house. Isabelle hung some of her posters too close to the Picconi's. I move them.

We've practiced and practiced and practiced. We've advertised. All that's left is to count the hours until Saturday.

16

Isabelle tiptoes out of her private dressing room—the bathroom. "Do I look all right?"

"You look great. How do I look?" I glance down at my legs and wish they were as tan as Isabelle's.

"You look great too. Are you nervous?"

"Not too much. But what if no one came other than our moms?"

"We'll find out now—it's show time!"

Isabelle and I are ready to perform in our matching black and red sequined costumes—the same ones we wore at the spring gymnastics recital. We're ready until we peek through the curtain.

"Look who's out there!" I point to two boys, arm wrestling on the bench. My left eye begins to twitch. Todd, the cutest, most popular boy going into sixth grade, is actually wrestling on *my* bench—on *my* property! I find it hard not to stare at his wavy blonde hair and blue eyes. I can't believe he's here to watch our show. I'll die if he laughs at us and tells everyone at school next week about our "stupid" show.

I'm wearing sequins and about to perform in front of Todd. It gets worse. He is sitting next to the infamous Jake the jerk who lives around the corner. Now my stomach is doing somersaults. Isabelle is a pale shade of green, a discouraging color.

"The Shining Stars—more like dull stars. This is going to stink." The boys stomp their feet and chant, "We want a show. We want a show."

This is not what we expected. Like our title, we expected stardom. While making the posters, we fantasized that a talent scout would drive by in a limousine and stop to gaze at our fabulous poster. He would be curious, hoping to find undiscovered talent. As soon as he saw us perform our first routine, he would be awestruck and anxious to manage us before another scout came along.

Unless one of those mothers sitting out there is a famous scout in disguise, I don't think we will be discovered today. Jake won't be awestruck either.

We cartwheel onto the driveway stage and try to forget about the boys. We worked too hard to chicken out now. With shaking hands, Isabelle and I lunge into a handstand and recite our introduction poem upside down:

"We are so glad you came today.

Take some time to rest from play.

While we dance and flip around,

Pray we don't fall on the ground.

Hope you like your candy bars,

And love the show

We're the Shining Stars!"

After the last verse, Isabelle and I land in a split. Thank God, some guests cheer and applaud. My pounding heart slows down a few beats. Of course the cheerers are mostly moms and their kids who still watch Sesame Street. Jake and Todd are too cool to clap. They mimic us and toss ripped up flyers into the air instead, confetti style. I wink at Laurie to trigger her memory, hoping she can read my lips mouthing *hurry up*. Her job is to hand out the candy bars to calm the crowd.

We wait, and wait, and wait. Everyone sounds impatient; even the animals are noisy. The robins sing. Becky's beagle howls. Crickets chirp. We forgot to rewind the tape after practicing yesterday. To stop the kids from fidgeting, Isabelle tells some jokes, "What is black and white and red all over?"

"A newspaper!" one of the boys shouts. "I hope she's better at gymnastics than she is at comedy."

I swear that tape rewinds in slow motion. Even our moms are chatting.

Click. *Yes!* The sound I've been waiting for kicks my body into motion. The audience stops wiggling for now.

We dance our first routine together, careful to hear our cue in the song and tumble across the lawn at the right beat. Now we're flowing like synchronized swimmers on land. Just as we turn round-offs into the last difficult trick at the end of the song, a slight timing error occurs. I taste the most unexpected flavor of Isabelle's foot landing on my mouth, squishing my head into the grass. Instead of doing a handspring over me, following my back walkover, she sprang right on top of me! I'm horrified, but the boys clap for more. Of course they're laughing like goofy idiots.

"Oh, no! Are you okay?" two familiar voices cry from the audience. Our moms could make this scene more embarrassing by running at us with Band-aids. Thank goodness, they stay in their seats.

I stand up and wipe the fresh cut grass off my hair. Isabelle gives me an apologetic and fearful look, probably because I'm ready to pounce on her.

The boys cheer even louder. "Awesome! Maybe we'll see some wrestling or at least some blood."

"Yeah … it might not be as bad as we thought!" Jake hollers and tosses more poster confetti.

The Dr. Pepper song begins. On with the show. Isabelle rushes into her solo routine, frazzled, but performs it perfectly. I watch her perform and can't help wondering why she has stronger muscles. We've both practiced the same amount for a whole summer, yet my arms look like noodles, and she looks like Nadia Comaneci, the gold medalist from Romania.

It's my turn to show what I can do. Two front walkovers into an almost split, three spins, getting dizzy, some dance moves to catch my breath. I turn and cartwheel into a back walkover. My head misses the ground by half an inch. Shimmy, shimmy, I circle my hips, and prepare for a running front handspring. But I have too much adrenalin running through me and land one foot in the shrubs at the end of the lawn. I turn around, leap twice, spin, and bow, ignoring the bloody scratch on my ankle. I did it! I finished my solo without totally embarrassing myself.

The audience claps again. I hope they're not just happy to leave.

The show ends just as the jingling ice-cream truck turns the corner—something more interesting to a bunch of hot kids who baked in the sun for forty minutes. I could go for a lemon Italian ice or a banana-fudge pop.

Todd walks off with Jake and says, "They should've wrestled."

Instead of hurrying across the street to get in line, Todd surprises me. "Here Francie, you look like you need something cold." He smiles and hands me three quarters.

My heart is pounding even harder now than during the routine. It's the first time I ever heard him say my name. Flattered that he even knows it, all I can think to say is, "Thanks."

As I wait in line, sparkly and barefoot, Michael appears. I want to cover my costume and run away, not have to explain the sequins. But there's nowhere to go.

"Hi." I smile.

Michael scowls.

"You can go ahead of me."

He stomps on my bare foot and orders two Bomb Pops. One must be for Randi. That reminds me I haven't seen her for a few days. Michael sticks out his tongue at me and marches back to his house. My stomach knots up again.

I slink back to my house with an unrewarding fudge pop, change into shorts and toss my costume in the closet and my pop in the trash. We practiced all summer, and it's over in a breeze. I probably hurt Randi in the process. The show was fun, but was it worth it?

17

If I wrote in a journal, today's page would be blank. I counted purple shirts and sketched the back of an old lady's head at church for an hour. Then I stared at a block of cheese for thirty minutes while Mom decided how much honey ham to buy from Fred-the-butcher, a friendly man with an Irish accent who likes to give me and Laurie free bologna slices. The highlight of the day was when Mom zoomed down the steep hill on Chestnut Street at fifty miles per hour, way over the limit, and missed squashing a squirrel by an inch.

The thrill and anticipation of our show is over. I don't need to practice gymnastics. It's cloudy, so I don't want to swim. I could go to Randi's, but what if she heard us doing the show yesterday? What if Michael squealed? How would I explain not telling her about it? I'd like to see her, so I decide to risk it.

Mrs. Picconi answers the door. Her face reminds me of Michael's scowl. "Come in. Randi's upstairs reading."

"Okay, thanks."

"You should be careful about hurting Randi's feelings. She already has enough heartache in her life. Between cancer and everything else at home, the last thing she needs is a friend she can't trust." Her words hit me between the eyes.

I nod. *Everything else*? What does she mean? This is not a good beginning. What state will Randi be in? Is she sad or angry with me? I climb the steps to Randi's room, and wait at the top, wishing I stayed home. Maybe a magic fairy will whisk me away. However, it's too late to turn around, and no fairy appears. I enter her room and greet the back of Randi, slumped over a torn piece of paper at her desk. Glitter dusts Randi's cheek, and the words *ing Stars* sparkle on the paper. This is not good.

I pick my favorite place, the rocking chair. It amazes me how much she sleeps since the tumors invaded her life. Her digital clock says 12:00, 12:10, 12:15. I rock back and forth, creaking a floor board and wondering if I should wake her or wait.

I tap her shoulder and whisper, "Randi. Randi … do you want me to leave?"

Randi slowly lifts her head off the book and looks directly into my eyes. An imprint on her cheek tells me she's been sleeping that way for a while. "Sorry. I didn't hear you come in, but I'm surprised. How did you find the time? You're such a busy friend."

"I'm not that busy."

"Were you sitting there long?"

"No. I just got here."

"Why did you come here today? Don't you have any more shows to do?" Randi looks out the window.

"No, yesterday's show was it. I came because I missed you this week."

"Yah, sure you missed me. You didn't even tell me you were having a show. No invitation. Nothing." She holds up the poster like evidence in a trial. "I wondered when you were gonna tell me."

"I was afraid it would upset you … since I … I did the show with Isabelle, and you couldn't be in it."

Randi's face is red. She smacks her desk with her fist. "Why couldn't I be in it? I can still do gymnastics better than both of you. I think you're embarrassed of me. You didn't want me in the show. You didn't even want me in the audience!"

"I … didn't think you could do gymnastics right now. I know you're better than me. I'm sorry. I don't know what else to say. "

"Just get out! Go play with Isabelle, your new best friend. I don't want to see you ever again!"

I bolt out of the room and run down the steps, skipping the last two. Randi's bedroom door slams behind me. I rush outside before Mrs. Picconi sees me leaving and tries to stop me. I sprint home. A jumble of thoughts race around my head: *I've never seen Randi so angry. I should have told Randi about the show. But she couldn't be in it, and what does she expect me to do, sit around and watch her sleep?*

My life just got worse. I can't talk to Randi, or Michael, or her parents. I can't even look at their house. No way. And I'm not going back there until she asks me over. She's so mad, maybe she never will.

Since it's Sunday, I can't hide. Both my parents are home, enjoying a peaceful moment, until I come barreling through the door, wiping my eyes and sniffling. They put down their coffee and newspapers. The inevitable questions follow. "What happened? Are you hurt? Did someone do something to you?"

I start at the beginning, and by the time I repeat Randi's angry "I never want to see you again," I'm sniffling harder. Mom's stifling hug doesn't help. Now I have to listen to their advice.

Mom's sure I should go right back to Randi. "Tell her how sorry you are. I'm sure she didn't mean what she said. She's going through such an awful time."

Dad thinks I should wait until tomorrow. "You should apologize, but give her some time to cool off."

"I'm not going back there unless she invites me over. Not today or tomorrow or ever. I'd rather play with Isabelle anyway and forget about Randi for a while."

With wrinkled foreheads, my parents are about to say something—something I'm sure I don't want to hear. I turn and run to my bedroom before they try to change my mind. I don't care if they're right.

Just as I slam my door, a summer storm begins to rumble. Lightning flashes through the clouds and a wall of rain pours down from the sky. I slam my window shut. Does God want to correct me too? Right now He sounds angry.

18

Twenty-one cars have passed the bus stop. Waiting alone for thirteen minutes feels more like thirteen hours. Are other kids as nervous about the first day of school? After the long, easy days of summer, water droplets form on my nose and hands when I think of who might be in my class. I could fill a bucket by now. With my luck, I'll have to square dance in gym class and share my clammy hands with some obnoxious boy like Jake. He'd probably shout a loud *yuck*!

My new outfit is sticking to my skin like wet plastic wrap. Why didn't I listen to the wise weatherman who claimed it would be hot and humid today and wear short sleeves? And I've added extra degrees thinking about school. Last night I carefully cut the tags off and laid the clothes on my dresser. I buried my nose in the pile and inhaled the fresh from Macy's cotton/polyester scent. I couldn't wait to wear my yellow flower trimmed vest and matching jeans in the morning. Now I have to suffer through today's heat wave.

Isabelle is walking toward the bus stop with Becky. They hang out together a lot because their parents are good friends. I drop my book bag on the ground, relax my shoulders, and crack my neck a few times while waiting for them to join me. Crickets chirp in the background, unaware that the first day of school isn't an occasion to sing. Isabelle wears a new long sleeve purple top with a ruffled collar. She must be sweating like a pig too.

Becky waves a green piece of paper. "Me and Isabelle are in the same class. Isn't that cool? We both have Mrs. Delaney, and I heard she's easy."

"Lucky you," I reply. "I have Mr. Fortelli."

Becky scrunches up her nose and shakes her head. "Oh, you poor girl. My brother had him. He's real tough."

"Great." I feel another drop of sweat forming on my upper lip.

Chatting about boys, TV shows, hairstyles, and clothes, I forget why we are standing on the corner until I hear the rumbling of the yellow dinosaur bus.

The dinosaur bus hisses as a lady with a white bun opens the doors like a mouth to devour us. We all hesitate, not wanting to be first. Stepping onto the bus is the end of summer.

"Hurry it up, girls. Don't want to be late your first day. And I'm not losing my job on account of your yapping." Our driver is so charming.

The bus jaws close and we're on our way. We ride with kids from fifth-grade up to high school. The high school kids get off at the middle school to change buses. I'm glad to see them go. Even though they scare me, I'd rather face them than Michael. He's on Laurie's bus this year. Maybe God helped me this time.

Randi still can't go to school. I feel bad for her, but I'm also relieved. Going to school is hard enough without worrying about who to sit next to each day. I don't know what I'd say to her since our blow up.

I scan the neat rows in my new classroom for a friend to sit next to. The longer I stand here, the redder my face flushes. No one greets me or even smiles. Some girls from last year's class, like Julie with her flowing blond curls and tight Gloria Vanderbilt jeans, act as if they've never seen me before. I glance down at my flowered vest and imitation jeans and figure out why.

My eyes focus on the last row. On Todd. My face heats up another hundred degrees. Todd is talking to a group of boys and swinging an invisible bat at the far end of the room. I won't be sitting over there—my secret would be out the first time I looked at him and turned into a tomato. Sitting next to any boy is out of the question. I'd never be able to concentrate. Instead, I find the nearest chair, wishing someone would tell Nina there was a mistake—that she is supposed to be in this class with her friend Francie. Fat chance.

Mr. Fortelli announces that he is going to assign seats in alphabetical order to make it easier to take attendance. The down side to ABC order is that *McLean* is always in the middle. I have to sit in the apple core of the classroom. I'd prefer a seat in the first or last row—as an Adams or a Zimmer—not in center where sharks can attack from all angles. Even though I'm not in the seat I would choose, at least assigned seating separates the cliques into individual islands. At least I'm not alone.

Todd Williams sits two rows to the right and three seats back. I won't be able to stare at him or know if he looks my way.

Todd's eyes are on me as I take my new seat, center stage. I can feel it. "Hey, it's Dr. Pepper girl!"

He grins, but I'm not sure if he's teasing me or he likes me. Is this wishful thinking? Am I in daydream land again? If I'm not mistaken, it looks like he's reenacting Isabelle's shoe landing in my face. The hysterical laughter from his gang is not a good sign. *Okay, time to stop caring about Todd. Don't look at him. Don't look at him.* I sit down and pretend to wipe some invisible fuzzy off my sleeve just to peek over my shoulder and look at …

Todd winks at me. I try to figure out the mixed messages when Mr. Fortelli interrupts my important thoughts.

"Class, settle down." Mr. Fortelli's voice is steady. Slam! He bangs the desk with his ruler. The class is silent. "Just wanted to make sure you're all paying attention. I expect every one of you to be quiet and alert. You don't want to miss any of my jokes."

Mr. Fortelli scares me. His angry black eyebrows and his towering height make him a cross between Goliath and the Grouch from *Sesame Street,* minus the green fur. His bulging eyes scan the room for rule-breakers—something easy to become since he has a million rules: no gum, no talking, no note passing, no slouching, and no daydreaming. He'd probably give a kid detention for sneezing too loud.

How hard is sixth grade going to be? More tests, more projects, more reports. "All to prepare you for junior high," explains Mr. Fortelli. No one here wants to *think* about doing junior-high work.

It's the third day of school and Mr. Fortelli has assigned our first project—an art contest. I break rule number five and daydream about winning the art contest, until I hear the words, "divide into groups and design a patriotic poster." I hate the word *group.* Why doesn't he just say find the clique you fit into, or don't. Non-clique types must remain alone and pretend they don't mind.

The clusters form around me but not with me, like blobs of oil repelled in a dish of water. I pretend to be busy searching for something in a folder, like I don't care and don't have tears to hold back, but I wonder, *what's wrong with me?* My chair is the only one occupied until Ann, a lanky girl with braces, approaches me and asks if I want to be in her group. I spring out of my chair, bumping my knee on the desk, and join her friends—the cluster of other misfits. Even though I don't fit into any group, I'm much more at ease with these girls who still wear bell-bottoms jeans than with the group of snobbish, Gloria Vanderbilt Jeans girls.

Ann has a great idea: we are going to paint the colors of the flag behind a black silhouette of a famous memorial, the statue of soldiers mounting the flag on Iwo Jima. Ann said she'd bring in the photo for us to copy. I offer to bring in the poster board, some glitter, and glue. Now I'm excited to work on this project. I made some friends and we have a plan for the assignment. I can show off my artistic ability, and maybe we'll win the contest.

19

I hum the song "Celebration" as I run home. It's Friday. Isabelle and I have planned our weekend together, swimming, swimming, and more swimming. We'll enjoy the last hot days of an Indian summer.

"Mom, can I go in Isabelle's pool?"

"Honey, I know you had a fight with Randi and said you don't want to see her again, but ... maybe you should since she's having surgery tomorrow. You'll feel better if you make up." Mom lays the invisible weight back onto my shoulders.

Couldn't Mom have given me a simple yes or no? "Okay fine. But I'm not changing out of my bathing suit. I'll just throw an outfit over this." I cross my fingers behind my back, hoping the cross will cover my lie.

I grab a towel and scoot out the door before Mom can see me run the opposite way. Instead of heading straight down the street to Isabelle's, I go the long way, around the block, to avoid passing Randi's house, to avoid her window and her eyes that may be looking out from behind the pink curtain. She told me to go away and never come back. She gave me permission to have Isabelle for my best friend. So why am I hiding?

Seeing Mrs. Picconi would be the worst. I don't want her to invite me in or chastise me again, and I don't want to apologize and be trapped in another game of tug-of-war between friends. It's much easier to have one friend and do what I want than to feel pulled in two directions until my heart has emotional blisters from the constant tugging.

I hug the curb along Chestnut Street, where cars race along like the Indy 500, and use it as a balance beam. As I turn the corner, the horrific sound of barking dogs gets louder. *Only two cute Chihuahuas. But why are they charging at me?* I believe they are harmless until they nip at my bare legs and bite my ankles. I scream, whip my towel at them and run away as some old hag in curlers calls them inside, a little too late.

By the time I reach Isabelle's house, I'm a mess. I rub the bloody scratches with my towel and wipe my eyes. I catch my breath at the curb for a minute. I hate dogs, and I hate being afraid to walk down my own street. I hate hiding from Randi.

Isabelle's Siamese kitten brushes against my sore leg. I like cats. Not too many are vicious, and their purr doesn't scare pedestrians to death.

"Hey, what happened to your legs?" asks Isabelle, opening the door for me.

"Those Chihuahuas around the block hate me."

"Why did you go that way?"

"I felt like running, that's all, but now I don't want to swim with my legs cut up. It'll sting."

We play Wiffle ball in the street instead. I run barefoot across the hot pavement and imagine a boundary line on Hartwell Drive I can't cross—in view of the Picconi's house.

If I keep moving, I forget—about Randi, about Todd's mysterious wink, about being an outcast. As I disappear into sports, nothing else matters.

Six o'clock. I was dreading this moment, when I have to decide which way to go back. If I go the long way, I might see the dogs. If I go straight home, I might see the Picconis. They don't have to say anything. I'll know what they're thinking.

I don't want to get bit by the evil Chihuahuas, so I run straight home.

It might be my imagination, this feeling that someone is watching from Randi's window. I can't resist the temptation to sneak a glance through the corner of my eye. It looks like the pink curtain moved. *Could the wind have blown it?* I run faster with my eyes focused on my front door.

What lousy timing! I have to stop and wait for Mr. Picconi to back his Corvette out of the driveway, because he's reversing and looking the other way. *Should I wave to him when he turns his head?* I guess I'll have to unless I can hide behind a few leaves.

Mr. Picconi looks left, then right—right at me. *Hey, who is that*? A stranger is driving the Corvette away. Should I call the police?

After stuffing the bloody towel into the bottom of the hamper, I greet Mom with fingers crossed again. "Randi was sleeping, so I went to Isabelle's house." The lie flows out too easily.

"She must've been sleep walking then, since I saw her get in the car with Rita just after you left," Mom says, folding her arms and arching her eyebrows.

"She must have woken up."

"What happened to your legs? You look like you were playing in a rosebush."

I give up. This lie is getting too complicated. "I went straight to Isabelle's—the long way, so you wouldn't see me."

"You could have told me you wanted to go to Isabelle's house instead. I'd understand."

You wouldn't. "Sorry I lied."

Mom pours hydrogen peroxide over my cuts.

"Ow! You could've warned me."

"It's just hard to see Randi go through this alone since you were such good friends. We've watched her grow up with you."

"I didn't want to go to Randi's house since she's mad at me. And Isabelle was waiting for me."

Mom doesn't say anything which makes me feel worse. Then I remember the car. "I forgot to tell you to call the police. A man stole Mr. Picconi's car!"

"No, honey. It wasn't stolen. They sold it."

"Why would he do that?"

"It's not our business. You should go do your homework while I finish cooking."

"Grrr." I run to my room and shut the door until we get on with our usual routine of dinner, showering, an episode of *Three's Company*, and bedtime reading.

I can't concentrate on my book. My parents' muffled voices are begging me to eavesdrop again. I creep over to their door that never closes properly and listen hard.

"I know. Rita was so upset. She told me she had no idea Sal missed so many days of work this year. And since he was fired, medical bills are piling up. They even had to sell his car. I'm worried about him."

Dad lets out a long sigh. "He's got to get it together, or it's going to get worse."

Before I go to sleep, after finishing a chapter of *Are You There God? It's Me, Margaret*, I remember to pray as I always do. Something awful might happen if I don't. I wonder if God minds that I pray at lightning speed and usually fall asleep before finishing. This time I add a prayer for Randi's operation—and her dad. Like Margaret in my new favorite book, I ask God, "Are you there and listening… if so please make Randi get better and make her cancer stay away this time. And God, I have one more request. Please give her a friend."

If Randi has another friend, I won't feel like a jerk. I repeat my prayers until they fade into dreams.

***

Tires screech … and smash! I wake up to a nightmare.

Dad's the first one out of bed. "What in the world?"

Mom comes out tying her robe. "What happened?"

Laurie and I lean against our bedroom doors, half-awake, waiting for an answer as Dad looks out the living room window.

Dad shakes his head as he opens the front door. "Sal crashed his car into our mailbox."

We watch from the den window as Dad helps Mr. Picconi out of the station wagon, which is hissing smoke and now has a dented front fender. It's hard to see the damage in the dim light of five o'clock AM. Mr. Picconi looks all right, except for the way he's walking with his arm slung over Dad's shoulders.

As my eyes are just getting heavy again, I hear Dad's voice in the next room. "He'll be fine after a few cups of coffee. Sal was actually laughing that he almost had to wave good-bye to two cars in one day. Our mailbox got the worst of it, thank God. He must have been out drinking all night."

This is serious so I try not to laugh, but the image of our crooked mailbox gives me giggles. What's wrong with me?

20

Hundreds of wet sneakers squeak down the hall. I follow the herd until I reach room 6B, Mr. Fortelli's farm for growing future scientists, doctors, teachers, and artists. My body sits still, but my heart is jumping. Today our class finds out who won the contest. The posters are hanging, and the one my group did looks much better than the others do. I turn back to see Ann smiling. I nod in silent agreement.

Someone knocks at the door. Mrs. Grims from 6A enters with her class following. They line the wall like they've entered a foreign country. I wave to Nina.

"Good morning, boys and girls." Mrs. Grims' voice is husky, and she peers over her rose tinted glasses. "We are here to congratulate the students who created the best poster." She maneuvers her way to the displays in the back of the classroom by squeezing her body through the maze of desks. The fat on her rear takes on a new shape, like Play-doh in a stencil.

I hold my breath in anticipation.

"The other sixth grade teachers and I were unanimous in our decision. Will the group who created this please come to the front of the room?" Mrs. Grims places a fire-engine red bow on our poster. Warm color rushes to my face as I join my group at the front of the class. Everyone claps—everyone except Julie and her pack of wolves. I ignore their rolling eyes. *Good ... be jealous.*

After lunch, on my way to my seat, I notice Todd smiling at me. Maybe he's happy my group won the contest. I smile back.

He points to the corner of his mouth. I instinctively lick my lips and taste chocolate. No, not a chocolate chip smeared on my face. I must look like an idiot! I'm never eating chocolate cookies again. How come no one else pointed it out to me? Did it *have* to be Todd? I sit down and try to forget about the chocolate smudge, but I daydream that the chocolate spreads like frosting until it covers my whole face. I'll never forget this embarrassing moment. Will Todd? Can he ever look at me without laughing at my chocolate smile?

"Can you believe I smiled at Todd with chocolate on my face? How humiliating!" I push my math homework aside. Boy talk is more fun than fractions.

Isabelle laughs and tries to top my embarrassing moment. "When my teacher called on me in class today, I was drawing hearts. She picked up the paper to look at it. The entire class could read what I wrote on the back of the page—more hearts with *Mike* inside. For the rest of the day, kids were whispering, 'Isabelle loves Mike.' The sad part is there are two ugly Mikes in my class who both think I like them."

Isabelle jumps off her bed to search for last year's yearbook. She finds it right on the top shelf of her closet, in a neat bin with last year's schoolwork. *Why do I pick neatniks for friends?*

We sit down on her bedroom rug, lean against her ruffled bedspread, and flip across last year's memories—but not our memories. The yearbook is filled with candid shots of the popular kids, smiling with arms wrapped around each other. They have better times to remember than the kids they torment. The yearbook committee—whomever they might be—must have decided photos like chubby James in his bowtie playing chess have no place among the Colgate smiles. I have a sudden urge to color mustaches on their grinning faces.

The pages stick together and release an odor like old bread as we open to the class photos. Isabelle turns to her picture and we chuckle. "How did I think pigtails with ribbons looked good?"

My picture is worse. I have a stiff smile. "Thanks a lot, Ms. Photographer, for parting my bangs in the middle so I look goofy."

After criticizing ourselves, Isabelle flips to Carson through Curry and sighs. "Ahh, Mike Cilano. He definitely gets a ten for that photo."

"Now let's find Todd." We stare. And stare. We stare as long as we want and dream. I love the yearbook—we can stare without anyone knowing.

"Another ten," we declare in unison.

"I think I'll give Mike a nickname. Spanish Spice, or Taco, or El Niño.

"Go with Taco. It's shorter." Isabelle jots it down.

"You should rename Todd. Prince Toad is a fitting name for a handsome English chap." Isabelle bows.

"No way!" When we finish renaming the boys, we move onto the girls, not to nickname, but to compare and envy. I would like to have Kelly's perfect golden hair, Amanda's brown eyes with long eyelashes, Lisa's cute pug nose, Maria's heart shaped mouth, and Julie's athletic body. Of course combining them would probably create the Hulk's sister. Still, we imagine the changes we wish we could make on ourselves. We imagine the changes it would have on our popularity. Boys might rate us a ten.

"I know something we can change," I announce. "Our names. I hate the name Francie." My mind flashes back to the birds at the hospital. The name Randi chose stuck with me. "You can call me … Danielle instead."

"That's a cool name. I want to be Kristin, like my brother's girlfriend."

"From now on we have to call each other by our new names, even at school."

"Okay, Danielle."

"I have to go home for dinner now. I'll see you tomorrow, Kristin."

I peddle home chanting, *Danielle McLean, Danielle McLean,* trying to get accustomed to the name I've given myself. I feel like a new person now. Francie was dull. From now on, I'm Danielle, free as a bird.

I drop my books on the kitchen table.

Mom is busy stirring something that smells like stew. "Did you have a good day, honey?"

"It was okay, I guess. My group won the poster contest." I sink low inside, remembering Julie's rolling eyes and the chocolate.

"That's great! I'd love to see it. This seems to be a good day for everyone. Mrs. Picconi says that Randi is doing well and is already out of the intensive care unit. She gets to come home sometime next week." Mom looks at me with her wide eyes and sweet smile.

"Maybe I'll visit her when she gets home." This pleases Mom, but I'm not sure I want to see Randi. It has been two weeks since she told me to go away. I have other friends now.

21

Now that the temperature has dropped, and it's too cold for Wiffle ball, "Kristin" and I have a new obsession—roller skating at Great Skates Roller Rink on Saturday afternoons.

After an hour with the phone attached to my ear, our chauffeur plans are made. Becky's mom is taking Krisitn, Becky, and me to Great Skates. Dad is picking us up. My parents bought me new skates with sparkly purple laces, and I'm wearing a new outfit I got for school—a pair of pink corduroy pants with a matching plaid blouse and a pink vest. The pants feel soft as kitten fur, the pastel colors complement my fair skin, and according to the experts in *Teen* magazine, pastels are "in."

According to Becky, who knows fashion, pastels are not in. She informs me of this the second I sit down in her truck. What if she's right, and my outfit is horrible? What if I'm the only girl over the age of two wearing pink pants? If so, I'll be the geek of the roller rink. Usually Isabelle (I mean Kristin) would say something nice. This time Kristin sits quietly while Becky gives me a fashion critique.

"Aren't you going to get hot wearing corduroys?"

"No," I answer, more like: "NNN-Ohw," with a southern drawl. But I do notice sweat trickling down the indentation of my backbone.

"You look like the Easter Bunny." Becky holds her fingers up like two rabbit ears. I'd like to say, *Better than a pig. Go away. Kristin and I are best friends.* But Isa--Kristin might stick up for Becky and make me look like a fool.

"Thanks. That's the look I was going for." I wish we could turn around and head home so I could change. Now the color pink is making me sick.

The long line we wait in weaves around the metal bars like amusement parks lines. It's just as thrilling as waiting for a giant rollercoaster. We can hear the music pound. It'll be our turn soon. Once inside, the doors shut, and a new atmosphere surrounds us—dark with rainbow lights that flicker and dance to the rhythm. We breathe in the excitement.

The rink reeks of freshly popped popcorn, chocolate candy, floor wax, and sweaty feet. I love the strange combination—the fragrance of fun.

While Becky and Kristin are busy adjusting leg warmers over their skates, I dash over to the bathroom to see how bad I look. Something must be wrong with me—I still like this outfit. Even though I think it fits me well, I will never wear it again. I don't want to hear any more jokes about my clothes, and I don't want to look like a dork. I'll have to wear a bodysuit, spandex tights, and leg warmers next time like all the good skaters do. Maybe taking the barrette out of my hair will help me look cooler. I apply some lip-gloss and comb my hair. No need for blush. I'm pink enough.

"Danielle, are you coming? You're taking way too long." Kristin rolls over to me and pulls my arm.

"Okay. I was just fixing my hair." I can't say I'm deciding if Becky was right about my pink pants.

As I enter the floor to skate, I sense all eyes are on me. They probably wonder why some girl is skating in an Easter bunny costume, especially since Christmas is in a few weeks. What was I thinking when I bought this outfit? It's going to be hard for me to have a good time skating today. My mind replays Becky's words like an annoying commercial stuck in my head.

After a few times around the rink, I manage to forget about what I'm wearing. Becky skates with me, so I can't look that bad. We hold hands, crossing them like a pretzel, and skate fast, bouncing to the beat of "Heart of Glass," my favorite Blondie song. Becky drags me around the turn faster than I'm able to skate on my own. Sometimes I miss crashing into the bars or another kid by a fraction of an inch—scary and thrilling at the same time. I'm glad she's strong and doesn't drop me. Sometimes Becky skates with Kristin. They make a better team. But then I'm left out, and feeling left out stinks like Swiss cheese.

Skating is fun, but we're motivated to skate for another reason. Boys. The first half of the session, we scope out who is cute and who can skate. We smile and roll by, hoping someone will ask us to skate for couple's only. I'm not too good at roller flirting. But maybe as Danielle—I could be.

Kristin leans toward me and shouts something during the girl's skate. "Look at who is standing near the snack bar."

I skate one way while my head stays fixed in the other direction. Our eyes lock. Whoa! Kristin pulls me into reality and out of the way of a wobbly skater I was just about to plow into.

"Thanks ... that was close! Wow! I can't believe he's here."

"I swear Prince Toad was staring at you!" she winks at me.

"No way. He could have been looking at anyone near me."

Kristin pulls me to the exit. "Come on ... let's go to the snack bar. Maybe he'll talk to you."

I follow her off, protesting. "No, I don't want to talk to him. I won't know what to say."

"Don't worry. I'll help you."

Just as I head into the snack bar, I feel a tap on my shoulders. My heart immediately leaps into my throat! I'm afraid to turn around.

A voice too high to be Todd's greets me. "Hi ... I didn't know you skate too. Who did you come with? Not Randi, right? She couldn't be well enough to skate if she can't even go to school." It's Kimmy. She blabs on and on, loud enough to be heard over the music. "So how is she? You still see her a lot? Too bad she's not in school. I heard she was going to be in my class again this year."

I don't know which question to answer first, and I'd rather not answer Kimmy at all. "Actually, I haven't seen her in a while." I'm not supposed to feel a flood of guilt. I'm Danielle. I came here to have a good time, not be reminded of …

Kristin interrupts and saves me from this conversation. "Can you come here? Becky wants to ask you something."

"Okay, I'm coming." I look to Kimmy. "I have to go. Maybe I'll see you later."

"Right, see ya later. And tell Randi I said hello when you see her."

Becky rolls her eyes at me as I slide next to her at the table. "What did she want?"

"Nothing—saying hi. She was in Randi's class."

"Oh."

Silence. I wonder if Kristin and Becky are thinking about Randi too. I fold my thoughts into a neat square and stuff them in my pocket.

"Let's skate. I'm—"

I'm incapable of speaking. I stand up and notice a pair of black skates in front of me. My eyes follow up the light blue jeans and glowing white t-shirt to Todd's face. He is standing two feet away from me. I think I'm going to pass out.

The lights have dimmed, and the music has slowed down. I forgot it was almost time for *couples skate*. Is he going to ask me? *Please. Please.*

22

Something must have happened between the time I smiled at Todd and when I bent down to tie my loose skate laces. Todd isn't in front of me anymore and neither is Kristin. They are skating hand in hand away from me. I can't believe it! I thought she was going to help me talk to him.

I want to curl up in a ball and cry, but Becky is standing next to me. Maybe I had it wrong. I do need Becky. She was just being honest about my clothes. Kristin is not acting like a friend.

"That stinks. I thought he was going to ask you to skate. Isabelle knows you like him." Becky says exactly what I was thinking.

"Oh well. Who cares? He's a terrible skater anyway." I wonder if I sound believable.

She tries to cheer me up. "I have an idea. Let's put our skates in the locker and go to Woolworths. I want to show you something."

"How can we leave?"

"We have a stamp on our hand, so they'll let us back inside."

We still have another hour left, so I say okay. Anything to get away. As we leave the pounding music behind, Becky whispers just loud enough for me to hear.

"You want to know how I got this new bracelet?"

"Wait … don't tell me. You found it in the closet with your other Christmas presents."

"Not quite. I gave myself an early present from Woolworths—for free! It was so easy. I just dropped it into my purse and walked out." Becky spins the fake pearl bracelet around her wrist. "Do you want to try? We could get makeup—that'll fit in our pocket books."

Becky shoplifts? Is she joking?

"But what happens if you get caught? Your dad's a policeman."

"That's exactly why I won't get in trouble. I'll just get a warning."

She's not joking. Be brave. Remember, you're Danielle now.

My eyes twitch as if protesting our plan as we walk into Woolworths. It's a jam-packed store with many aisles and everything from clothing to gardening supplies. If I take one lipstick, it will be like taking a shell from the ocean. Who would notice?

Becky instructs me on how to look natural. "Don't take too long picking something out. After you drop it in your purse, keep looking at things like you haven't decided what to buy. And don't look away from the salespeople. Just smile at them or ask them where to find the birthday cards." Becky leads the way to the makeup department. "Come on, talk to me about school or something."

It's hard for me to think about anything other than how I ended up here. Ten minutes ago, I was in Great Skates, now I'm shoplifting at Woolworths. If I knew the day would turn out like this, I would have stayed home to watch Laurie practice baton twirling.

However, I'm Danielle, and this should be easy. We browse through the clothing aisle, holding up a shirt here and there. I smell perfume, a lot of perfume, an overpowering field of wildflowers. My eyes water.

The lipsticks and eye shadow come in so many shades like Dad's pastels. Rows of browns, reds, and pinks. I'm amazed at how many different colors you can paint your lips. My hands tremble as I try to read the labels. I choose *Perfectly Pink* and drop it in my bag. Wandering in circles, I glance at the mirror on the side of an aisle. My whole face is perfectly pink!

Becky nods at me—my cue to walk away. How does she look so calm? I'm afraid I'm going to set off an alarm when I exit through the electric doors. I pass one salesperson, a tall woman with frizzy salt-and-pepper hair wearing the red Woolworths vest and hanging cheap sweaters. I don't want to ask her anything. Signs point the way to the cards. So, without asking for help, I find the stationery aisle and pretend to hunt for the ideal birthday card. The doors to freedom are not too far away. I follow the arrows to get out like I would through a carnival haunted house. If I can reach the exit sign without a Dracula security guard stopping me, I'll be able to breathe again.

Stepping outside, I expect to hear sirens. I'm a thief. I stole a lipstick. Becky is waiting by the curb. All we need now is a getaway car, if we could drive.

"What took you so long?"

"I read about twenty 'Happy Birthday Mom' cards like you told me to."

"See how easy that was."

"Yeah, sure." *Easy for her to say*. "We better get back to the rink before Isabelle starts looking for us."

At the rink, Isabelle is not looking for us. She's sitting cozy next to Todd. I think I'm going to be sick.

"Becky, can you go get you-know-who? My dad's gonna be here any minute, and I don't want to talk to that ... that bimbo. I'm not calling her Kristin anymore. Kristin is too good for her."

"Why don't we just leave her here?"

"I'd like to, but I'd have to explain everything to my dad. He would make me go get her anyway."

"Okay, I'll get her. I know a name to call her that she hates even more than Isabelle."

I wait around the corner, within earshot, and peek over the divider.

Becky takes Isabelle's arm and pulls her up. "It's time to go … *Dizzy Izzy*."

"You mean Kristin." Isabelle throws Becky a fierce look.

"No, Dizzy fits."

I chuckle.

After Isabelle changes out of her skates, which seems to take longer than usual, she meets us outside. But I don't look at her. I shiver and stare at the sliver of a moon while we wait for our ride.

"Are you mad at me for skating with Todd?"

"Of course not!" I look in my pocket book. The silver lipstick tube shines back at me.

"He asked me to skate to talk about something. He wanted to know how my brother was doing. He saw Joey limp off the field at the last football game of the season. So I told him how he sprained his foot, and he's been treating me like his slave." Isabelle grins.

"Oh." *I don't care.*

"He asked if I could get time off from Master Joey and go to the movies with him one day over vacation. I told him I had to ask you first, cuz it might bother you."

"Are you kidding? You said that. Now he'll think I like him."

"Well, don't you?"

"No! Go ahead. Go to the game. He's not my boyfriend. Why should I care?"

"Good. Cuz I'm dying to go with him."

My dad pulls up in the squash car. It stinks of cigarettes, so I crank down the window and let the cold fresh air pour in. I don't know what to think of Isabelle. I'm still angry, but I'm even more embarrassed. What if Todd tells his friends what Isabelle said? I can hear the teasing now. "Francie likes Todd!" I was hoping the new year would bring me a new body and a new boyfriend. In four days, it will be 1980. I doubt that's enough time to turn into Barbie and meet Ken. I'm hopeless.

Laurie cuddles under a brown throw blanket. "*Little House on the Praire* is on—it just started."

"Good. Is it the one when their mom gets deathly ill during a storm?"

"No. You'll see."

I hope it's an older episode when Laura Ingalls was a kid in school fighting with bullies.

I settle into the couch, so warm and comfortable, and rest my head on the padded arm of the plaid sofa. I'm Laura Ingalls for an hour on a hot summer day in Walnut Grove, Minnesota, even if the window behind me declares Long Island cold with flurries.

Laura likes a boy, but he's not interested. He likes Mary, her sister. One hundred years ago and all she needs is a pair of roller skates to be me. Different year, same problems—

boys and lack of curves. I want to scream *stop! Don't do it!* Laura stuffs two apples in her shirt. I wince when she writes on the chalkboard and the apples drop to the floor. How could she think that would work! How could I think Todd would want to skate with me when Isabelle is pretty with curves, and I dress like the Easter bunny! I hope I never have to live through another embarrassing moment like that again. At least *my* life's worst moments can't be seen on channel 10 reruns.

23

I don't need to turn around, though I'm tempted to sneak a glance at him. Even in a noisy classroom, I hear Todd's voice. In fact, he must be talking extra loud on purpose, especially when he emphasizes the name Isabelle.

"I went skating over the break. A lot of cute girls hang out there. Blah, blah, blah. Isabelle. Blah, blah, blah."

Why can't one of the cute girls he talks about be Danielle, or even Francie? It's stupid to care since he was a jerk to Isabelle too. He took someone else to the movies the night they were supposed to go. I can't be mad at Isabelle. We're both on the same side now—hating Todd and liking Todd. Maybe it was just "Kristin" who was a jerk, and it was my friend, Isabelle, who apologized. It's a good thing she did. I need the few friends I've got. I can't imagine life without friends. Like Randi. *Not again.* I push that thought to the back of my mind before it takes root.

Mr. Fortelli wastes no time getting back to schoolwork. "Vacation is over," he announces as everyone settles down. "We've got a lot of work to cover from now until spring. Today, you'll write an essay on how inflation and the oil crisis are affecting people around our nation as we begin a new decade."

A few kids groan. Is everyone like me—sick of that word "inflation" that keeps popping up at the dinner table, on the news, and in the classroom? To me, it means I can't have designer jeans.

I stare at the clock, counting how many times my stomach grumbles in a minute, and waiting for the end of the day.

I swear someone's eyes are burning a hole in my back. Are they Todd's eyes? I have an idea. I can take out the pocket mirror from my bag and check the faces behind me. Slowly, trying not to attract any attention, I slip out the mirror while Mr. Fortelli writes the homework assignment on the board. I tilt the mirror at just the right angle. Todd's face fills the frame.

He winks.

The mirror smashes on the floor! All eyes are on me now.

Mr. Fortelli whips around as if a gun went off and looks directly at the broken pieces under my desk. "You don't need a mirror in school. Your mind should focus on learning not vanity." He points to the dustpan by the closet. "I hope you don't believe in bad luck."

"Sorry. It slipped when I took a pencil out." I hurry to clean up the mess with my head down. Bad luck seems to be following me.

Chuckles fill the room, but not for long. The clanging bell blasts away all sarcasm. That bell is the best sound in the world.

Nina opens the drawer to her snack heaven. I choose a chocolate-covered cupcake with a stripe of white icing across the middle. Nina picks a glazed donut. We slide the piles of newspapers and ashtrays off her shiny black coffee table to make room for a napkin, and then kneel down to feast and watch *General Hospital*.

"My mom doesn't care about junk piles, but you should see her explode over crumbs! So be neat. She'll kill me if she has to vacuum!"

A loud plunking sound comes from the corner of her den. Droplets of water fall into a metal bowl like notes from a tin instrument. A circular yellow stain on the ceiling marks the entrance point like a bull's eye. Nina picks up the full bowl, empties it in the sink, and puts the bowl back under the drip.

"It's too bad we don't have a dog. Wouldn't this be a cool way to give him water? Here Fido...drink up. Or, I could measure rainfall for a science project."

I laugh, but inside I feel sorry for her. Nina jokes about her house slowly falling apart as if it's an aging lady. But the lady didn't start aging until Mr. Sanchez moved out.

"Hey, my mom left her cigarettes here. You want to try them?"

I'm not sure if she's kidding, so I'm not sure how to answer. I don't want to sound like a goody-goody. What would Danielle say? Danielle would be cool, and I have to be cool. "Sure … I'll try one." I wait to see if Nina means it. "Have you ever tried smoking?"

"Nah…I hate when my mom fogs up the house. I'm curious why she thinks they're so great. She's gotta smoke with her Cheerios. Heck, she won't even get out of bed without lighting up. I can't imagine how she can ruin a delicious ice cream cone smoking between licks. That's just wrong!" Nina opens up her freezer. "Hey, wait a minute. Maybe that's not such a bad idea. Let's get some mint chocolate chip ice cream to wash down the bad taste."

In a few seconds, she holds the lighter flame to the end of a Marlboro Light with a heaping bowl of green ice cream in front of her. She coughs and holds the lighter to my cigarette. I take a deep drag and explode in a coughing fit. It's the worst thing I've ever tasted or breathed! I grab my bowl of ice cream. The cool fresh mint puts out the fire raging down my throat. *Why don't we stop?* We continue this routine, daring each other to finish the cigarette to see who could smoke more. Inhale smoke, cough smoke, and swallow ice cream. By the time I take my last puff, I'm racing to the bathroom to puke.

Nina calls through the door, "Are you okay?"

Hunched over the toilet and staring into a mint green pool, I answer, "I'm better now, but I don't want to smoke anymore."

"Me neither."

We both chew bubble gum.

Nina opens some windows, letting in a dusting of rain and snow. I place the box of cigarettes exactly where I remember seeing it. Nina often jokes at school about her mother's temper, telling me what set her off *this time*. I have trouble believing her mom has an angry side. She hugged me like a long lost relative. Nina must be exaggerating. She's probably just worried about getting in trouble.

As soon as we hear the car in the driveway, we close the windows, leap on the couch and put on our innocent faces. Mrs. Sanchez comes in speaking Spanish, and I don't understand anything until I hear, "Did you do your homework yet?"

Nina looks at me with a fish face. "I was just about to—"

"Hey, what happen to my cigarettes? I know this pack was missing one, the one I had at breakfast, but where's the rest? Nina, get your butt over here and tell me what happen!"

I've never been so happy to see Mom's headlights. I huff into my hand to test my breath. It smells like peppermint. I jump in the car, but before we back out of the driveway, I can hear yelling coming from Nina's house. The front door slams shut. Maybe Nina wasn't exaggerating.

Now that the closed door muffles the screaming, Mom reverses and gives me a look.

"What was that all about?"

I shrug my shoulders.

141

Mom drives at a sloth's pace through the slippery mix of freezing rain and snow, a winter storm that is worse than predicted. Tree branches bow under the weight of the slush and surrender to the storm. Mom seems concerned with not smashing the car into a pole like she did during another icy storm years ago, not about my afternoon at Nina's.

Smoke spirals from the chimney next door to ours. As Mom eases into the white-blanketed driveway, my eyes drift from the gray puffs down to Randi's pink curtain, the room I'm usually so careful *not* to see. The storm and the darkness hide me, so I stare. The curtain is slightly parted in the middle. A light is on. Are there eyes behind the curtain? Is Randi watching the outside world—the world that she used to be a part of?

The fabric moves ever so slightly. I'd rather think it was the wind or even a ghost moving the curtain. I'm afraid if I stare too long, it will open all the way, and I will be staring into her face. As long as the curtain stays closed, her story stays behind it.

Will there ever be a day I don't have to avoid the pink curtain—a day I don't care who's behind it?

24

Water drips in quarter notes like a distant drum beat. Drip, two, three, four, drip, two, three, four, drip. I yank the covers over my head to hide from the blank face that floats above me without a body. It stares at me with a pleasant smile … it spins and spins, twisting until the mouth opens wide to scream. The face comes closer, enlarging, like a balloon about to burst. Before it's close enough to identify or pop, I open my eyes. I've had this dream before. Now in the darkness, I lie, soaked in sweat, listening to the trickle of icicles melting and splattering against something, like a drippy faucet.

I try my hardest to picture the face. As usual, I can't. It could be Randi watching me, or Julie mocking me with her eyes, or even an angel warning me. Whoever it is leaves me in a heavy, creepy fog. I'd like to stay in my bed, sulk, or lift my spirits with a carton of vanilla ice cream. But I can't. One quarter of school is left, which I don't want to mess up. Besides, we're out of ice cream. With these thoughts, I motivate myself to roll out of bed.

While eating Golden Grahams cereal and finishing up my math homework, I doodle the name Danielle on my notebook in puffy, bubble letters. I'm going to change my name today in school. It will be my own experiment. Will Danielle be treated better than Francie?

On the bus, I show Isabelle my bubble letter artwork. "I'm going to change my name officially to Danielle today in school."

"You are? How?"

"I'll write Danielle on all of my papers. If Mr. Fortelli asks me why I am not writing Francie, I'll tell him Danielle is my real name."

The bus screeches to a stop at the curb. "Bye, Kr... hm hmm." I clear my throat, unable to croak out Kristin. I don't want to remember the Kristin from the roller rink, the Kristin who almost let a boy get between us. Or did I let a boy get between us?

"Bye, Danielle. See ya later."

I already notice a few curious glances.

Everyone stares at the blackboard. Mr. Fortelli has drawn the words "1980 Olympics in Moscow" in a circle with a red diagonal line going through it. He hands out copies of an article from this morning's newspaper. *President Carter declares the U.S. will boycott the Olympics as a protest to the Soviet Union's invasion of Afghanistan.*

Sighs and comments rattle through the room. I'm disappointed too. I was looking forward to watching the gymnasts with Isabelle.

"Your assignment is to read the article, summarize it, and write a closing paragraph with your opinion and response to the article." Mr. Fortelli's forehead has more wrinkles today.

As the class writes, Mr. Fortelli reads today's *Newsday*, shaking his head.

"Hi!" I tap Isabelle on the shoulder and surprise her as she lifts a forkful of cafeteria food to her mouth.

"Hey! Don't scare me like that. I almost dropped the beef slop. I've been craving it all morning. Nothin's better than yesterday's burgers, chopped up into macaroni and fake cheese," says Isabelle.

"I'll stick with peanut butter. So did you write Kristin on your work this morning?"

"Uh ... not exactly. How 'bout you?"

"I wrote Danielle on every paper I had—a math quiz, a map, a drawing, and an essay about the Olympics being boycotted."

Just as the peanut butter begins to slide down my throat…RING! I jump out of my skin. They need to lower the volume on the bell. It's a miracle I haven't choked to death.

Isabelle seems to be in a hurry. "Maybe I'll write Kristin on my homework—at least on the scrap paper. See ya."

Lunch break always ends before I'm done eating. I swallow the last of my chocolate milk in one gulp and wipe the mustache off. "See ya."

Just as I stand up to throw my garbage away, I feel a familiar tap on my shoulder, like a porcupine poking me. It's smiling, overly peppy Kimmy.

"Hi, Francie. I wanted to ask you a question."

This would be a perfect time to say I'm not Francie, I'm Danielle, and walk away. But I don't. "Sure. What is it?"

"Have you seen Randi lately?"

"No, why?"

"I heard from my sister's friend who was hanging out with someone from your block that she saw Randi. She said Randi got huge, went from super-thin to super-fat in like a week ... blew up like a blimp. Is it true?"

"I don't know. Like I said, I haven't seen her. I've been busy." I can't help scrunching my nose and rolling my eyes, even flaring my nostrils a bit. Kimmy must be able to see the disgust on my face. She gets defensive.

"Hey, I didn't say it. I'm just repeating what my sister's friend said. I hoped it wasn't true."

"She must be exaggerating or just mean. What an awful thing to say!"

I walk away from Kimmy. That girl is worse than a porcupine. Whatever she says stabs all the way through me. Now I can't get the blimp image out of my head.

Back in class, every student has a graded math quiz lying on the desk, every student except me. Mr. Fortelli leans against the first desk in the middle row, my row. He is holding a piece of paper above his head. His face wears a scowl, a serious scowl.

"I was perplexed this afternoon as I graded your papers. It seems we have a new student with us. Does anyone here know a Danielle?"

Everyone wags their heads no, including me. I shrug my shoulders, wishing I was a bird that could fly far away.

"Let me explain how easy it is to become a detective around here. By the process of elimination, I have figured out who this mysterious person is." Mr. Fortelli steps toward me and places my test on my desk in slow motion. "Miss Danielle, in class you will use the name on the roster so there's no confusion. Understand? Does *everyone* understand?" asks Mr. Fortelli, increasing his volume from three to eight.

 I nod with quivering lips. The class nods along with me. More laughter comes from the back of the room. Who is laughing? Whoever it is, I wish they'd get in trouble for it— but Mr. Fortelli doesn't say anything to them. I'm today's lucky target for his dart throwing.

It doesn't matter that I got a 92 on the test or that he wrote, "Great job—whoever you are." I'd love to stand on my desk and shout "My teacher's a jerk!"

The rest of the day drags. The hands of the clock are stuck on two-ten.

The last thirty minutes crawl on until the bell clangs, finally. I sling my backpack over my shoulder, almost whacking Julie in the face.

"Watch it, *Danielle*! Danielle … how stupid," Julie whispers just loud enough for me to hear. As I make my way to the bus, my new name echoes through the hall. Am I imagining it or is everyone from my class retelling the story to someone else?

I slump into the seat next to Isabelle. "Don't even ask!" Isabelle offers me some pretzels, but I can't eat—my stomach hurts too much.

My experiment flopped. I wish changing me was as easy as writing a new name.

The bus turns the corner onto Hartwell Drive at the same time Mrs. Picconi pulls into her driveway. It's inevitable that we see each other since we live next door. Nothing but a row of bushes separates our houses, not acres of farmland or forest.

I stare at the bushes. When I stare, I remember how I picked blackberries that grow wild on their side of those bushes. Randi and I raced to pick the most until our hands were purple and covered with scratches. At my kitchen table, we poured the berries into bowls and sloshed them in milk to eat like cereal. We looked a mess, in stained shirts, but the taste was worth it. I miss those days.

Mrs. Picconi opens the car door and helps Randi out. At least I assume it is Randi because of the scarf on her head. My heart thuds like a dull drum. She isn't the skinny, active girl I was friends with and picture in my mind. She *has* gained a lot of weight and seems to be having trouble moving. I haven't seen her for so long. The change in Randi shocks me, even with Kimmy's gossipy warning.

She must feel me staring at her. Randi lifts her head and looks over at me. I smile and force my hand to wave. My mouth is paralyzed, unable to form any words. Randi waves back, but not a cheerful, happy-to-see-you wave, more of a sad wave—a wish-you-hadn't-ruined-my-life wave. She doesn't have anything to say to me either. I run into the house, passing Mom as she goes outside to talk with Mrs. Picconi—not a place I want to be. They haven't been talking as much since Randi and I drifted apart. I guess it must be awkward for them too.

I wait for Mom to come back inside and almost fall asleep with my head on the kitchen table.

"What did you talk about with Mrs. Picconi?" I ask, afraid to hear, but too curious not to ask.

"Well, she explained that Randi has gained a lot of weight, a side effect of the medicine she is on combined with depression. She still feels dizzy spells, headaches, and fatigue. They just came back from having more tests in Manhattan to determine what further treatment she needs.

Mrs. Picconi seems so discouraged. This cycle has been going on for a long time. Maybe you should go see Randi tomorrow."

Oh no. Here she goes again with the pressure and the guilt trip.

"I can't," I snap. "I already have plans to go roller-skating with Isabelle and Becky tomorrow." Mom's face sags and says it all.

"Okay, but the longer you wait, the harder it will be to go over there. I won't push you. I just don't want you to regret your decision someday. Summer is almost here. Do you realize it's been almost a year since you last talked with Randi or fought with her—or whatever happened to ruin your friendship?

This conversation needed to end. "I promise I'll see her another day this week."

Another day this week doesn't happen and another year of school will be over in less than two months. I think my friendship with Randi is permanently over too. My parents have stopped nudging me to visit her. My stubbornness is stronger than their hopes. It would be way too strange to show up at her door after a year of ignoring her. I doubt if she'd welcome me in. Some days I even forget to hide from her pink curtain.

25

I miss having one best friend and doing everything together. Now I have to compete to make Isabelle and Becky like me more than they like each other. I hate being the one left out, and I am already. Isabelle and Becky are going to the same expensive teen travel camp this summer. I can't admit to them that I'm going to the cheap day camp at the elementary school with Nina. I'll have to pretend I'm babysitting Laurie a lot.

After waiting until 11:00 a.m., the time my parents consider a reasonable time to ring a friend's house on a Saturday morning, I call Becky. Her mom says she's not there—she slept over at Isabelle's last night. Why didn't they invite me? I don't care. I'll just ask Becky to come to the mall and not Isabelle. Becky can help me choose trendy summer outfits to buy with my birthday money.

I dial Isabelle's number, but when her mom answers the phone, I ask to speak with Becky.

"Hold on. She's right here," says Mrs. Torelli.

I hear bacon sizzling and Isabelle and Becky giggling in the background. *What's so funny?*

Becky sounds surprised to get a phone call at Isabelle's. "Hello?"

"It's Francie. I was wondering if you want to go to the mall."

"Yeah, I'll come. Sounds fun."

I knew she couldn't say no to a day at the mall. Becky crunches on what I'm guessing is a strip of bacon. I grin because I can hear Isabelle complaining in the background.

"I thought you were coming to the beach."

"I need to get my dad a present," Becky says in a muffled voice away from the receiver. "Francie, let's check out Woolworths like the last time. I need some things there."

There is a huge Woolworths in the mall. A monster compared to the one by Great Skates. I get what she's planning, so I decide to bring my big pocketbook—just in case.

We air out the steaming car while waiting for Becky. Mom hands me fifteen dollars. "After I drop you and Becky off, I have to take your sister to baton twirling lessons. You said Becky's mom agreed to pick you up?"

"Mm hm. She said she'll pick us up in two hours." I walk outside as I answer. "Here comes Becky now."

"Okay. I guess that's all right. Make sure you both stay together and don't talk to strangers."

"Come on, Mom. I think we've heard the 'don't talk to strangers' speech before!"

The line at the gas station is eight cars long. Mom grumbles about the skyrocketing price of gas. Becky and I mumble in the backseat.

"Could it get any hotter in this car?" Becky asks.

"Only if we were driving on the equator."

"Once the traffic lets up, we'll get a breeze," chirps Mom.

"Becky's mom is going to be waiting to pick us up before we even get there."

"I know. We should have gone twenty minutes the other way to Cedar Beach instead," Becky groans. "Isabelle's going down to Cedar today in her air conditioned car. We could have gone with her."

One strike against me and one point for Isabelle.

"I'd rather hang out in an air-conditioned mall than walk on the rocks and pointy shells to get down to the water. The Sound has no waves. It's boring, not worth the pain."

"True."

One point for me.

For the rest of the drive we silently endure the heat, which casts a sleepy spell over both of us, like the field of poppies in *The Wizard of Oz*.

At the Smithhaven Mall we get out of the car oven and step into a frigid Macys. Becky and I say, "Ahh," together.

"Look, goosebumps." I hold out my arms for proof.

Now that we've cooled off, we wander in and out of various stores, not buying anything, until we're drawn to Tom

McCann shoes. Becky insists I spend all my money on a pair of leather sandals since they look cool and feel comfortable. I convince her to buy the pair of thin-strapped red sandals she tried on as she sashays around the store.

On the way to Woolworth's, we devise a plan, a shoplifting competition to see who can snatch the most. Most of me is a wimp who doesn't want to take the chance of getting in trouble. Part of me thinks it's wrong because God is watching me. All of me wants Becky to like me more than she likes Isabelle. I have to do this.

Becky instructs me. "Go in first to the right. I'll go through the music department. When you're done, meet me outside the other exit by JC Penney's."

I forget all Becky's previous advice about looking inconspicuous. I enter the store with guilt written all over me, heart racing, cheeks flushed, avoiding eye contact with any sales person.

I see something I like and want: a cool pair of sunglasses with silver frames. They fit easily in my bag. I slip them in and cover them with a tissue. One thing is enough for me, so I browse the aisles, leading myself toward the exit. Who cares if Becky wins the game? At least free shopping (that sounds better to me than shoplifting) is getting easier. Maybe there is still some Danielle in me. I can't wait to try on the sunglasses.

I notice Becky, who nods, and we meet by the next store. My heart begins to slow down again, but I'm excited to show Becky my great new grab.

"Can I show you what I got?"

"In a minute. When we get … "

I feel a heavy tap on my shoulder. Please be a kind mother telling me to tie my shoe, or a girl scout asking if I'd like to buy some cookies, or even Kimmy tapping harder than usual.

"Girls, come with us willingly, and we won't have to use these." A security guard shows us a set of handcuffs. We follow.

My heart rate has just doubled and my chest pounds like a time bomb. Is Becky nervous? People are staring, hopefully no one I know. It would be just my luck to see Todd strut down the hall.

I don't know where they are taking us. Are the police going to take us away?

As if the guard heard my thoughts he explains, "We're taking you to the office to have a talk and call your parents. I think you know why. You were being watched on the store cameras."

That lump in my throat is back. *Was God watching me too? Are the guards his angels in disguise?* We climb a narrow staircase and enter a closet-size room without any windows. Is this a jail? The musty room is bare except for an empty metal desk, four chairs, and a Woolworth-framed picture of a sailboat on the wall. It has probably been there since the store first opened. I want to sail away on that faded boat. I'm afraid to look at the guard's face. I'm afraid to look at Becky too. For the moment, I don't care if she likes me.

A police officer comes in the room and one of the security guards leaves. "Here, write down your name, address, phone number, and your parents' names."

Mom said not to speak to strangers. I don't want to say anything. I wish I could write the name Danielle, tell them this isn't the real me, and give a phony phone number. But I'd get in more trouble, I'm sure. They'd probably send me to a nut house.

The policeman stares down at us. His head nearly touches the ceiling. "We're calling your parents. They'll be coming up to this room so we can discuss what you've been up to. While we're waiting, you can dump your bags on the desk."

My hands shake as I dump out my pocketbook. Coins rattle against the metal desk. My *Perfectly Pink* lipstick rolls across and drops on the floor. A circular red tag dangles from the center of the silver glasses like a drop of blood.

Becky's bag is even noisier. A compact mirror with blush spills open, leaving a trail of pink powder crumbs. A few lipsticks roll out. A chain necklace, two bottles of nail polish, and a watch crash onto the desk. Becky slumps back in her seat, shaking the empty sac emphatically. She doesn't look scared, just angry that she was caught. She would have won our competition for sure.

This has to be a nightmare. I can't believe I'm in trouble with the police. I can't believe there's no air conditioning in here. I'm sweating like the boys in gym class. This place smells like a locker room.

I search the walls for a poster: *Make the prisoners suffer; they'll confess*. If this were a dream, the poster would be there. It isn't.

The sunglasses look cheap under florescent lights, and I don't want them anymore. Becky's face is reflected but distorted within the frames. She wears a stubborn frown, and she's not crying. My whole body hiccups with held back tears. This stinks! What a horrible way to spend a beautiful summer day! We should've gone to Cedar.

Thirty minutes later the door opens, and our parents squeeze into the narrow room—all four of them, each with a wrinkled forehead. They line up against the wall with tight lips and shaking heads. Could they look any more disappointed? I wonder if this is how a prisoner feels when visitors come to the jail. I feel like a slimy ball of dirt. I need a shower.

As if on cue, tears begin washing my face as I twiddle my fingers in circles. The police officer tells our parents what we've done and shows our loot.

Becky's parents yell at her all the way to the mall exit. They apparently don't care a bit if the whole world knows their daughter is a criminal. My parents give me the "just you wait" look. This should be a fun ride home. At least *my* dad's not a cop. *Poor Becky.*

The front seat doors slam. In the privacy of our squash car, Dad lets loose.

"How could you do such a thing? We thought you could be trusted. We thought you were smarter than this. Are you trying to ruin your life?" They both have their heads turned toward me, waiting for my answer.

I shake my head no between sniffles and hiccups.

"Well, you're grounded for a month, and no roller-skating." Dad turns around and starts the car up. "I'm so disappointed in you."

His words stab me. How long will it take him to forget what I did? If I know Dad, he'll make sure he remembers for at least the month I'm grounded. One month. Four weeks. Thirty-one days. Half my summer is wiped away for a stupid pair of sunglasses.

26

How do I describe my summer vacation so far? I'd like to say same as last summer: swimming in Isabelle's pool, practicing gymnastics, and roller-skating every Saturday. Doing nothing would be okay if I chose to do nothing, but being grounded and forced to do nothing is the worst kind of nothing. I'm going to explode with any more nothingness!

My one escape is summer camp in the morning. Dad decided I should still be allowed to go to camp, partly because they already paid for it—no matter how cheap the camp—and partly because Mom works part time at the senior center four days a week. Dad made sure to emphasize his distrust in me.

"We can't trust you to stay home to watch your sister until you prove yourself. So as soon as you set foot off the bus, you'll march straight inside."

Every day, come 12:30, I rediscover my wallpaper. I lie on my bed, stare at the stripes of flowers on my wall until the rows that were messed up stand out. Having nothing better to do, I continue the search for other seams to see if they line up right. The perfectly aligned flowers alternate directions, dancing their way to the ceiling. The messed up row of flowers ram into one another, and fight their way to the top.

Hours of TV would help if I wasn't memorizing reruns. I like drawing, but not when I can hear kids playing outside. Every so often, I peek out the window to see who's walking by. *How is Becky surviving her punishment?*

I am going stir-crazy to the point of digging out my dusty diary, removing the cobwebs, and actually writing about my life behind flowered bars. Words circle inside my head that won't come out of my mouth, but flow through my pen.

Dear Diary sounds too corny, so I just vent my random thoughts

The ceiling is spinning. If I stare at one of the dots, the rest move and I get dizzy. This is what I do to pass the time. I know it's my own fault. I stole a pair of sunglasses and got caught by the security guard. The tap on my shoulder was the worst. I felt scared and foolish and slimy following the guard. Stealing was a dumb idea. Not cool.

Why did I listen to Becky? I knew stealing was wrong even if I didn't get caught. Why did I want to be someone else? And who was I trying to be? I thought if I changed the outside, gave myself a new name, I'd be transformed. But it wasn't that simple.

Danielle is not adventurous, or cool, or brave. She's stupid for following. I'm stupid for following, and I'm not Danielle. I'm still Francie whether I like it or not. Not.

Mom says God still loves me and will forgive me when I confess what I did wrong, but I'm afraid he's going to punish me too. What could be worse than spending half my summer staring at the ceiling? If God is going to discipline me, I hope it happens outside—because one more beautiful day stuck in my room, and I'll scream. Is this what it's like for Randi? Confined to a prison at home? Except she doesn't deserve her prison walls.

I ruined my summer. I ruined my summer. I ruined my summer. But I won't ruin my life. My shoplifting days are over. Can my punishment be over too—for good behavior?

While being cooped up, I have one fear: what if Becky's punishment is over and she is back to hanging out with Isabelle? The time I am away, they could be together. They might be having so much fun that they don't even miss me. I don't want Becky to take my place as best friend to Isabelle. Then all I'd have to hang out with is my cat. Nina is great, but she's too far away to see every day. Oreo would have to be my best friend. I had better keep my two-legged friends so I don't turn into a crazy lady who talks to animals and starts resembling them.

On Saturday, my first day out since that horrible day at the mall, I slip into my bathing suit and dash over to

Isabelle's without even bothering to call. The scent of freshly cut grass never smelled so wonderful.

Isabelle opens the door, dressed in her pajamas.

"Hey, you're free! I'll go get in my bathing suit."

Becky comes down the stairs, also dressed in pajamas.

Just great.

"Hi Francie. So you're not punished anymore?"

"No. The wardens finally let me go. If I had one more day, I think I would have died of boredom. My parents totally overreacted."

"My parents let me out after two weeks."

"Two weeks? You're lucky." *What's wrong with my parents?*

"I definitely learned a lesson. I'll never steal in department stores with cameras. Next time I'll check first."

I hope Becky's kidding. She can't be that stupid.

For the rest of the summer, our friendship becomes more of a tug-of-war. Becky, Isabelle, and I each try to pull the other to her own side. I'm a step away from losing a friend, again.

Friendship with Randi was never a struggle. Like two years ago when I got to sleep on Randi's boat. This was one of my best summers. We fished, swam, played cards, and ate fried flounder. The harbor at Cedar Beach was so peaceful. Sleeping to the gentle rocking of the boat soothed me like a lullaby. I wonder if Randi still goes out on their boat. I haven't noticed it lately on the side of their house, so it could be at the harbor ... or maybe they had to sell the boat too. Actually, I can hardly picture their house at all—as if now it's invisible on Hartwell Drive. I'm too busy struggling to keep my new friends to notice much of anything. I hope Isabelle and Becky stop pulling against me. I'm tired.

27

August passed like a summer storm. I get angry all over again when I think about what I did to lose the month of July. Now it's September. How depressing.

At the bus stop, Becky, Isabelle, and I work on a plan to deal with the seat problem we are going to face as soon as the bus pulls up.

Isabelle asks, "Who should sit next to who on the bus?"

Becky has the best idea. "Why don't we switch off?" She points to me. "You can ride with Isabelle today, morning and afternoon. Tomorrow Isabelle rides with me, and I'll ride with you the next day. We'll repeat the pattern every day."

Seems like my absence didn't ruin my chances at all. "Sounds good to me."

"Sounds good to me too." Isabelle puts her hand out for us to pile our hands on. Our pact reminds me of a stack of pancakes. I must be hungry.

I'm glad I'm not sitting alone on the bus for my first day of seventh grade. I'm already worrying about everything that could possibly go wrong. I could trip as I walk into the classroom and knock a tooth out. I could split my pants and expose my flowered underwear. I could get lost in the building and miss every class. I could turn strawberry red as I repeat my name three times for the teacher to hear it correctly.

"You want to know how I woke up this morning?" asks Isabelle.

I nod.

"In the middle of a dream about racing Becky to school, I heard this scratching sound. I was sure a thief was opening the door until Penny meowed."

Isabelle chats about her new Siamese kitten as she bites her nails down to the skin. I try my hardest to listen to her tale of Penny's adventures, but school jitters clutter my mind.

Isabelle lifts her sleeve to show the bloody stripes.

Showing me her scratches brings me back to the moment until my thoughts drift again. New grade, new school, even a new, unfinished building. The teachers' voices are going to have to compete with power drills and hammers. I bet everyone in school will fail the hearing test.

Walking down the crowded halls to find my first class makes me claustrophobic. All the voices mesh together like a swarm of bees—until the power drills start and cover all sounds.

Are all junior high teachers as strange as the ones I have? My math teacher resembles a frightened sparrow with her pointy nose and high-pitched voice, fluttering about the classroom nervously. I can handle the pre-algebra problems, but I can't handle the voice—a rusty door hinge swinging back and forth in my ears. She contributes to the noise pollution.

My history teacher wears her long, frizzy-blond hair pulled back in a ponytail, and doesn't look that much older than the ninth graders. She dresses as if she is ready for a safari hike in her camouflage pants and boots.

"I hope you all love history! I'm Ms. Sullivan, and I promise to do my best to convince you history can be fun." She crosses her heart and ducks behind her desk. Up she pops wearing a President Nixon mask. Her odd personality reminds me of Mr. Picconi.

She points to a chart of the three branches of government and asks in a Nixon-imitation voice, "Who knows the Republican presidential candidate running against Jimmy Carter?"

Silence.

"I guess it's been a long summer. It may take a while to get your brains functioning again. Knock, knock, knock." She pretends to knock on Todd's head, just the place I happen to be staring. "I think I heard a squirrel whisper the answer. Yes, Mr. Squirrel is right. Ronald Reagan." She switches to a President Carter mask. "You can expect to do a lot of research in my class before the election." She takes off her mask. "Voting is one of the greatest privileges we have in this country."

A few groans. Not many future politicians in this group, I guess.

Taking notes in her class is a challenge. She is a fast-talker, hard to keep up with, and overly enthusiastic about maps. Who gets excited over maps? I'm afraid she's going to call on me. I think my eyes are getting worse. I can hardly tell if she is pointing to South America or Africa.

My book bag hides my glasses. I thought the blue, marble-looking frames were nice when I picked them out. Now I'm not so sure. Since Todd's in my history class, I squint a lot. If the teacher writes in yellow chalk or my seat is too far back, I'm forced to find my glasses. Not to put them on, though. I hold them up, glance through them, and put them down. It takes longer to copy the notes that way.

The first two days of school were bearable, except for the homework. Does every teacher have to assign work the same day? By the third day, it is obvious that seventh grade is going to be hard. Ms. Sullivan, the strange safari teacher has won another title—Queen of the Quiz. Imagine giving a pop quiz the first week! Pop quizzes might even be worse than dividing into groups.

The one good thing about taking a quiz in history was Todd talking to me. "Whoa! That was unexpected," he said. "Wonder what made her do that to us the first week of school?"

I smiled back, trying to look comfortable talking with the cutest guy in school. No big deal. I always get clammy hands and tongue-tied. Why couldn't I have said something funny like Nina would have?

I follow Isabelle's steps onto the bus, so close that her hair swings into my face. She follows Becky. As I wander down the aisle of seats, my book bag bangs into every seat, causing my ruler to poke me in the ribs. I wish Isabelle would pick one of the first seats so I could sit down with her and stop the painful jabs. She takes her time, passing every seat, and sits in the last row, but next to Becky. *Wasn't today my turn to sit with Isabelle again?*

"Pick a seat or move over!" Jake shouts from behind me. If I wasn't afraid he'd hit me, I'd tell him his breath stinks.

I take a seat in front of from them and look out the window, listening to them talk and laugh. Maybe they forgot about the order. I could say something, but what? *You're in my seat. It's my day to sit with Isabelle.* Anything I say would sound stupid, so I keep my mouth shut.

The next day begins the way the previous one ended. This must be a joke, and my friends are getting ready to say, "We fooled you!" Becky is sitting next to Isabelle again. Do I smell? Do I have stinky breath? They open their notebooks as I pass by them. Maybe they just need to study for a test together since they are in the same class.

No, the ride home makes it definite. They're not going to sit with me anymore. This is no joke!

"Here, Becky, sit next to me," says Isabelle in a louder than usual voice. "Isn't it interesting that Kimmy asked us why we didn't go to day camp with *Francie* and Nina?"

"I know, especially since *Francie* had to baby-sit all day long and couldn't go to our camp. Maybe she should change her name again to Francesca. She'll be talking in Spanish soon."

Isabelle and Becky laugh and act as if I'm invisible. Are they mad at me for being friends with Nina and telling them one little lie? I got bumped to lower than three in our crowd. *Now what?*

Before the bus even comes to a stop at my street, I grab my book bag and make my way to the front of the bus, trying to keep my balance, trying not to cry. I don't look back.

28

"How was your day?" Mom sniffles and forces a smile from behind a tissue.

"I'm too tired to talk about it." I try to smile back.

I wish Mom would stop watching soap operas. They make her cry every time, which she forever denies, claiming her allergies are bothering her again.

"Francie, I need to talk to you and Laurie about something important after Laurie comes in and gets settled. Her bus should be here any minute now."

"I'll go do my homework in my room." Today I don't mind staying in all afternoon doing homework. I have nowhere else to go and no friends to see.

My room is a mess—the mess I left in my rush to get to school this morning. Many mistrial outfits lay tossed on my unmade bed, attempting to reach the ceiling. Socks adorn my desk searching for their proper match. Earrings dance in a random design across my dresser, and shoes lay scattered across the floor for anyone entering to weave around the obstacle course. No welcome sign here. The reek of dirty socks, a similar smell to popcorn, keeps everyone out. Cleaning is a foreign word in my room, but I might as well get a head start. Mom's important talk is probably to complain about my pigsty and assign some new chores like she does every fall. Where do I begin? From the bottom up or top down?

I make my bed first so I can lie on it without climbing the clothes mountain. Now it looks inviting. Maybe if I lie down and rest for a while, I'll have more energy to finish cleaning. I close my eyes and snuggle under my cool satin blanket, wrapped around me like a caterpillar in its chrysalis.

Someone knocks at the camper door. I wish they'd go away. It could be a woodpecker. I open my eyes, expecting to see flowering trees, but orange and yellow flowers decorate the wall, not a forest. Someone won't stop knocking.

"Francie, are you awake? Laurie's home. Can you come here for a minute?"

"I'm coming." I drag myself out of bed, wishing I could go back to camping dreams instead of hearing a speech about pitching in more around the house.

Laurie is sitting on the couch chewing what is left of her fingernails. She looks cute in her pigtails. Mom isn't even there. "Where's Mom? I thought she wanted me."

"I don't know. She said she'd be right back. This is boring."

I hope Mom hurries back before Laurie starts chewing her toenails. Did she call us out here to practice her disappearing act? "Hey, Mom! We're waiting!" Five minutes have passed.

"I'm right here," Mom answers, instantly appearing from around the brick wall. She needs to work on that part of her act.

Mom sits down on the loveseat across from us and blows her nose again, making us wait another minute. I focus on her long eyelashes, wondering if it's painful for her to curl them.

She takes a deep breath and leans forward. I suddenly suspect this isn't about chores.

"The reason I wanted to talk to you is that Mrs. Picconi told me some bad news today about Randi." Mom's eyes start filling up as she struggles to get the words out. "She has been getting worse. The cancer spread ... and her doctor estimates ... she…she might have about six months to live at the most."

Laurie whimpers and starts to cry. I'm not able to make a sound. My throat is tied in a knot. Six months? Less than a year? At eleven years old? Randi was supposed to get better. She was supposed to ride her bike again. She was supposed to be able to do gymnastics again. I was supposed to be her best friend again, wasn't I?

Mom gets up and comes to the couch, hugging Laurie and me at the same time. She locks her arms around me, squeezing me hard, until the sobs break past the knot in my throat.

Mom won't loosen her arms, so I can't run away and be alone. We cry together. Hearing my mother cry makes it harder to stop. We stay that way until my neck aches from the strained position and there are no more tears left.

Drifting down the hall in my numb body, I pass by the portrait my father did of Randi when she was nine, before her life—and my life—changed. I stare at the pencil strokes, imagining how Dad followed each curve of her face and put it to paper. The image captures a moment of her life—she was fidgety, posing for those ten minutes. I remember how anxious we were for Dad to finish the drawing so we could run in the sprinklers. She didn't know she had only a few years left to live. Neither did I.

On my clean bed, I collapse. My body feels like cement. I'm unable to lift my head or arms or even a finger. Guilt is my blanket. An ache pierces through me, more painful than anything I can remember, as I realize how I abandoned Randi. I tried so hard not to think about her this year, to have fun and forget about what I did. The excuse that I didn't know this would happen seems so lame. I knew she was suffering and didn't have any other friends, yet I left her anyway.

Will I ever be able to see her again—to tell her how sorry I am, how I have missed her, how special she is, and how I wish we could go back in time and change everything that has happened? As if Randi's angels are whispering in my ear, calling me over, I feel drawn to Randi's house. I have to go see her and become her friend again, before it's too late.

29

My heart pounds harder than ever as I lift my finger toward the doorbell and hold it an inch away, frozen. I close my eyes and press it. The chimes ring inside the house, and ring inside me too. I hate being an unwelcome surprise. That's what I dread the most—seeing the shocked look on the face of whoever opens the door.

Somehow, I got up the courage to walk over here. It's too late to turn around—now that I hear footsteps coming to answer the door.

"Oh ... hi, Francie," says Mrs. Picconi, looking shocked as I expected.

"Hi. Um ... could I come in and see Randi?"

Mrs. Picconi steps outside letting the door shut behind her. I forget how to speak.

"I think she'd like to see you. However, before I say yes, I need to explain some things to you. Did your parents tell you how sick she is?"

I look down and nod, barely able to breathe.

"Francie." Mrs. Picconi waits until I look at her. As always, she is open and honest. "We decided not to tell Randi. Knowing would do her more harm than good." She pauses, and I wonder how much longer she'll keep me outside. "Since she may not have that much longer, you can't come in and out of her life again. I just *can't* watch her get hurt a second time. Please decide now if you're going to be her friend or not."

Somehow I keep my eyes on her sad face. "I am," I choke out.

"I'm glad. She needs a friend more than medicine. Wait here for a minute while I talk to Randi."

Another minute to shiver and sweat while I listen to the drum of my heartbeat speeding up. My teeth chatter, clapping to the rhythm.

Mrs. Picconi comes back and holds the door open to my second chance. The house smells of matzo ball soup, a welcoming aroma that gives me hope—hope that Randi will also welcome me.

If I have to look at Mrs. Picconi one more second, I'll burst into tears. I practically fly up the stairs to get away from her. I am not sure who is hardest to face—Mrs. Picconi, Randi, or my own guilt.

The green-carpeted stairs, the cream walls, the black-and-white drawing of an old-fashioned train framed in black, and the wooden sign reading *Randi's Room* flood my mind with memories. Making crafts; playing board games; watching Randi's mom braid her hair and fix it with ribbons; searching for Randi's first missing tooth she dropped; having our first sleep-over in sleeping bags in her living room; playing in Michael's room with his matchbox car collection. How many times did I follow Randi's steps to her room upstairs as we talked and laughed all the way? I used to be so comfortable being here—the exact opposite of how I feel now.

I knock on her door, unsure of what to expect. It's been over a year.

"Come in." Randi's voice sounds slightly deeper than I remember.

A drowsy, different-looking Randi raises herself in bed onto her elbow. Her Barbie doll face is now white as blank paper and swollen from the weight she gained. Her eyes and nose seem lost in her puffy round cheeks. Most of her hair is growing back, but it's not the silky golden brown hair from before. It's short enough for the army, dark, and coarse. What's happened to her? Everything lovely about Randi has been stolen by this horrible disease, the cancer thief. It even took her shine.

"Why are you here?"

"I ... I don't know. It's just that ... I've been thinking about you. I want to be friends again."

"Don't you have other friends?"

"Mm hm." I nod. "But that doesn't matter."

Randi moves her mouth into that Mona Lisa smile. Or is it a frown? Is she still angry? I can't read her face. My one advantage is knowing how much she needs a friend.

"I'm surprised. I don't know—"

"Can I stay and play a game or something? Please?"

"I guess so. For a little while. I've nothing better to do. I've had nothing to do for over a year."

Ouch! *I'm a lousy friend.*

Pretending I'm not astonished at her face and hair is hard, even with all my practice at fibbing. What should I say? I show up out of nowhere for no good reason. I see that she looks completely different, but I don't say anything about it. *God, I need your help. Please give me the right words.*

I'm sure I hear the words: "Say you're sorry," so I go for it.

While Randi hands out the cards, I stumble over the first words that come to mind. "I know it might not seem like it, but I've missed you. I'd really like to be friends again. Sorry I was such a jerk."

Randi is silent for too many seconds. I count and hold my breath as if I'm underwater. "You hurt me over a year ago, so it'll be hard to call you a true friend. I mean—I don't know if I can trust you after you lied and kept secrets behind my back. You can come over if you want, but I'm not promising ..." Her voice fades into a quiet sniffle.

I nod.

"I still don't feel good enough to go over your house. I get tired lately—probably from the medicine I'm on—so if you do want to be my friend you'll have to come to my house."

I can't look at her yet. *How could I have abandoned such a truly nice person?*

"I'll try to come over three or four days a week, as often as I can. I'm getting a ton of homework now."

"Well, you'll have to promise me you're gonna act like a friend. I don't want to get hurt again."

Now I remember how much Randi is like her mom, straightforward, honest, and sincere. Unlike me. I wouldn't blame her for hating me and telling me to go away. I have to be a true friend to her for whatever time she has left. Maybe God will give her more time if I pray for her every night as I go to bed.

I look straight at her. "I promise."

This is a promise I intend to keep.

"Another thing about my medicine ..." Randi hesitates for a moment. "Is that it makes me fat. I can't wait until I can stop taking it. I hate looking like this, but I can't help it. Please don't tell anyone how fat I am."

"I wouldn't talk about you. I'll never hurt your feelings again." That pain is back in my throat again, holding back the tears. I don't like knowing what she doesn't know. Another secret.

We play card games for a while until Michael peeks his head in. "Hi. Do you want to play cars with me?" He looks a bit surprised to see me in Randi's room, but smiles anyway. I wonder if he knows how sick Randi is. *God, please don't take his sister away.* I hope the doctors are wrong and she surprises them by living to the age of eighty.

178

Randi shakes her head. "Maybe later. I'm getting tired. Sorry." She looks to me. "Francie, do you think you can come over tomorrow after you get home from school?"

"I'm sure I can. Tomorrow is Friday so my homework can wait."

"Good. See you tomorrow." As I turn to walk away, Randi adds, "I *am* glad you came over."

"I am too." I run down the stairs and yell, "Goodbye, Mrs. Picconi. Thanks," to be polite. But I shut the door before she can say anything else.

Outside, the cool evening air slaps against my bare arms. When I came over it was warm enough to wear a sleeveless top. But even in the coolness, I sweat as I race home. So many emotions run through me. I'm happy and relieved that I can be her friend again, but now I can't hide from the hurt I caused her. What did I gain by ignoring her this last year? If I knew earlier how little time Randi might have, maybe I would have valued her friendship more, been kinder, more understanding. Maybe I would have cared a bit less about me.

Facing death changes how I see everything.

30

I find myself alone on the bus again, staring out the steamy window, and thinking about Randi. I have done a 360-degree turn in my relationships. Randi is my friend again, and I'm not talking to Isabelle or Becky. The tradeoff happened the same day.

Even my view of the kids on the bus has changed. Each pair of eyes hides a story I'll never know, just as they'll never know the story I'm hiding. And they probably don't care.

Behind my blank face is an alarm clock, set for six months from now. A month has passed, but my clock hands stand still. I want to stop time. I watch the numbers and wonder if the date has already been set by God. Six months of school can drag on endlessly, but six months to live? It becomes a fraction of a second that slips through my hands like melted butter. I wish I didn't have to waste some of those hours at school. I feel robbed of my time—time left with Randi.

Week after week, I've been going through the motions of junior high life, but I can't focus on the lessons. Especially grammar. What did Mrs. Block say the difference was between direct objects and predicate nouns? I'm focused on my own topic: what should I talk about with Randi today?

She might not like hearing about school since she can't go. But what do we have in common now?

During the break between classes, Nina nudges me in the hallway. "Hey, girl. Haven't seen you in a while. Where you been hiding? I have news to tell."

I've been avoiding Nina since I found out about Randi. I just couldn't get the words out. "I hope your news is better than mine."

Nina gives me a weird look but goes on. "Guess who was talking about you today?"

"Who?" I'm curious but still feel numb inside. Nothing could be more important than Randi dying.

"Todd! I overheard him talking to Mike. They were naming the good-looking girls in school. So of course, I was interested in what names came up. Todd said, 'Francie in my history class is real cute, kinda quiet, but cute.' I swear he said that!"

"No way!" I feel one-step higher than numb.

"Well, it's true. So what was your news?"

I can't look at Nina, so I look at my fingernails. "You know Randi, my friend next door. She has only—only—about six months left to live."

Nina looks spooked like she saw a ghost. "That's horrible. I can't ..." Kids rush between us as the bell rings, and I rush to my next class, leaving Nina in mid-sentence. I couldn't admit that she might have only five months left now.

Ms. Sullivan paces around the room asking questions about last night's debate between Carter and Reagan. She tries to light a spark in us, but everyone looks like they took sleeping pills. I hope she doesn't call on me. Dad made me watch the debate, but all I saw was Reagan's wrinkles as I tried to imagine what he looked like as a young actor. I only look at Todd once.

I throw my books on the couch, hug Mom, and dash back out. I don't want to waste any time answering Mom's questions about my day. Randi needs me. And I need her.

A plump woman with speckled gray hair answers the door. "Hi, are you Randi's friend?"

"Yes, I'm Francie." *Not Danielle.* "May I come in to see Randi?" As I am asking, she is already holding the door open and escorting me in. I follow this strange woman who is close to my height.

"I'm Miss Barbara, Randi's nurse. She's told me a lot about you. She was hoping you'd come today."

Although she hasn't said more than a few sentences, I can tell she's a sweet person. Rosy apple cheeks form when she smiles. Like Mrs. Claus! No wonder I feel so welcomed by her. I'm curious to hear her laugh. Does she sound like Santa's wife in the Rudolph cartoon?

Miss Barbara brings me into the den where Randi lounges on the couch and watches TV. "Look who's here!" she announces.

"Hey, you came." Randi shuts off the commercial for Crest toothpaste.

"Said I would ... so what were you watching?"

"Josie and the Pussycats—but I'm tired of watching. School would be more fun."

"Hey! You mean to tell me I'm not the most entertaining nurse around?" Miss Barbara winks.

"You know what I mean. These stupid cartoons have been on for three hours," Randi snaps.

"Randi, Randi, I'm just joking." Miss Barbara wraps her arm around Randi's shoulder.

"I'm sorry. You *are* the best nurse. I just want to do more than sit around and feel tired."

I'm surprised at how Randi reacted to Miss Barbara. She's not so easygoing anymore. I guess losing two years of her childhood could be the reason.

Randi sits on the same black leather couch in a room that hasn't changed at all. The television sits in the same corner. The white brick fireplace is still there but unused, not giving any warmth to the room that smells of fake pine and disinfectant spray. The caricature drawing of the family, done on their trip to Disneyland, hangs on the wall in memory of a happy time when Randi was healthy. That drawing is of the other Randi, the one I used to know.

Randi and I work on a puzzle of two Golden Retriever puppies resting in the grass. We are both quiet at first, until we watch the after-school special movie about a poor twelve-year-old orphan girl who moves in with her stuffy, rich relatives and disrupts their lifestyle—a Cinderella story that has us laughing. I love to hear Randi laugh.

Miss Barbara serves us some hot cocoa along with Randi's afternoon dose of medicine. As Randi takes the pills, I wonder how they help her. Gaining six months of life isn't enough help. And what's the point if she has to spend those months tired and puffed-up? I wish I could stop these thoughts, but every time I look at Randi, thoughts of death invade my headspace and I can't blow them away like the meteors in the Asteroids game.

The movie is back on and I'm laughing again at the pranks the orphan pulls on her prim and proper relatives. I'm laughing, but Randi is sound asleep with her head on the arm of the couch.

Miss Barbara tiptoes into the room. "Randi gets tired when she takes her medicine. It also makes her a little snippy, so don't be offended. You made her day by coming over again." Miss Barbara wipes the tear from her eye, and grins. "But you might as well go home now. She'll probably sleep for a while."

"Okay. Please tell Randi I said good-bye and I'll come over tomorrow."

"She has to go into the city tomorrow to see her doctor. Maybe the next day would be better."

"You can tell her I'll come by either Sunday or Monday. I just want her to know I am definitely coming back."

I want to say something to Randi, even though she is sleeping. I'm afraid if I don't, I may never get another chance. I wait until Miss Barbara goes upstairs and out of sight.

"Good-bye, Randi."

31

It's that bothersome time of year, as Eeyore the depressed donkey would say. The last of the leaves waves good-bye to the trees and joins the colorful carpet on the ground. I have to gobble my breakfast because Dad will storm through the door, peeved that Laurie and I aren't out there raking. Even Mom finds extra chores to do around the house to avoid raking day. What I hate the most about this outdoor job is picking up the wet leaves with bugs hiding on them. What I hate second is how much time it takes. Our lawn is huge—four sections framed with giant oaks that scatter their dead leaves everywhere, as if on purpose, to laugh at me on raking day. Only the willow waves like he's sorry.

As I drag the bent metal rake through the leaves, it scratches the slate path, creating the sound of nails dragging on a chalkboard. How could Randi have enjoyed doing this? I look toward the Picconi's house and notice that no one has raked their leaves yet. The Picconis are usually the first to rise on Hartwell Drive—rising with the sun to gather the golden piles. Randi and Michael usually dive into leaf mountains before most kids roll out of bed. Now a thick quilt of leaves spreads across their lawn. I imagine the trees cried and knit the blanket with their colorful tears.

Dad also stops raking for a moment to stare. Is he angry because their leaves are going to blow over to our lawn? Please tell me he's not going to knock on the Picconi's door to scold them for their neglect.

He walks toward their house, but not to their door. Instead, he begins to rake the layers of leaves into piles. A wave of love and admiration for my father rushes through me. I decide to help him, hoping they won't look out the window and see us on their lawn. I'd rather it be a mystery or a surprise. We work quietly and contentedly. I don't mind the cold breeze whipping my neck or numbing my toes.

While busy on Randi's lawn, I reminisce with my father about fun times I had with Randi. "Before we bagged the leaves, we used to have races, jumping into the piles at the end. The first one covered in leaves won."

"Randi would knock on the door, before you were even awake. You had no problem running out when *she* asked you to help." Dad squints at me with a smirk on his face, forming a comical dimple on his left cheek.

"Well, Randi made it into a game, and at least I was with her. It was never my favorite thing to do."

"No kidding?" Dad exaggerates a surprised look. I love his silly faces.

"Another thing Randi and Michael would do was have a contest to see who could find the biggest worm. That was definitely not my favorite game!"

"Laurie would've liked that one. Remember when she brought a bucket of inchworms home? Your mom nearly fainted!" Dad stops raking for a moment and chuckles. "You never liked bugs—even the spider from 'Little Miss Muffet' scared you."

"Ha ha, Dad." I've heard that joke before.

"It looks like we're almost finished here."

"Can I go see Randi when we're done?"

"Sure, after you clean yourself up. And thanks for helping." He kisses my forehead.

I look around at the job we did. Without the colorful leaves, the trees look scary, and Hartwell Drive looks gloomy. I can't wait for the colors of spring, or even some snow to add a little sparkle.

Raking doesn't seem to be such a rotten job now that I'm finished and sipping a steaming cup of hot cocoa. I wipe my lips, throw my coat on, and head over to Randi's. On the way, I stop and gather a Ziploc bag of leaves we missed. Randi will love these. I know she'll have an idea for this sack of colored jewels. Maybe we'll decorate the castle walls or knit a magic carpet and fly over the rooftops.

32

Mrs. Picconi opens the door for me and I hurry into their warm home. My shoes are wet, so I step out of them just inside the door and run for the den.

But running on a newly waxed floor is not smart. "Whoa!" I shout as I slip and land flat on my bottom. I quickly stand up and gather the leaves that spilled.

Randi bursts out laughing at my unexpected greeting. "Are you okay? Your tush must be sore."

Her mom rushes in too. "Are you okay?"

I nod, rub my bruised leg, and hand Randi the leaves. "Here, I brought these."

"Neat, we can make leaf prints on handmade cards. Just don't slip again."

The smile on my face travels down to my toes as I watch Randi laugh. Randi's face lights up at the thought of creating a project, like I knew it would. It spurs me on to think of ideas. Everything seems possible—even designing a time machine for Randi to reverse her steps and stop whatever got her sick.

We empty the crisp leaves on her kitchen table and form a mosaic of color. The earthy smell fills the air as if we were covering ourselves in the fallen leaves under the open sky.

Randi's mom brings out some paper, crayons, glitter and glue, the missing ingredients to our artwork recipe. We concentrate on our work and don't say much to each other, other than to ask for a different color or to comment on each other's work. An hour later our clothes smell like leaves and twinkle from glitter.

When we finish, Mrs. Picconi displays our artwork on the refrigerator using apple magnets. "Very nice," she says.

We both smile. Maybe I'll frame the collage and hang it on my wall.

Randi cleans up the mess without being told. Of course, I help. But at home, I would have left it there until someone complained, or Mom bribed me with dessert. Sometimes Randi is the same Randi. *How does she do it? Would I be the same going through all this?*

While we work, Mrs. Picconi clears off the kitchen counter. She moves a few homemade decorations and sets Randi's framed school photo on the table near us.

"Mom, please get rid of that picture. It's not me."

In the photo, Randi wears a black velvet dress with a white lace collar. Her smile could make anyone smile. I remember when she first showed me her pretty picture on the bus ride home a couple of years ago. Compared to her photo, mine was pathetic. My hair was parted down the middle, a style unflattering to my round face, thanks to the photographer's assistant who enjoyed making me look as ugly as possible. I told Randi, "That's nice." Then I stuffed my photos in my backpack until I could bury them in an old toy box. Mom thought I lost them on the bus.

"It's still you," I mumble, not so sure.

Randi shakes her head. "Thanks, but I know I'll never look like that again. I hate it."

I don't say anything and would love to change the subject. Mrs. Picconi, who was silent during this conversation, wipes her eyes as she wipes the counter. Does she feel the way I do? I like seeing the picture when I walk through their kitchen. It helps me remember Randi the way she was before. Otherwise, I might forget how she looked when she was happy and we were best friends. It gives me hope.

I can hardly remember the girl in the photo, the healthy girl. What would she be like if she weren't sick? Would she be the best in gymnastics class or the smartest girl in her grade? Would teachers … and boys pay attention to her because of her sweet smile and long eyelashes? Would I be jealous of her now instead of sorry for her?

A funny story might cheer her up.

"Remember that silly photo I took with my family on Thanksgiving? All my relatives lined up for the picture— aunts, uncles, cousins—and for some reason I decided to scrunch my face up to see if my top lip could reach my nose. It could! My dad was so angry when he saw it. Now that stupid picture is hanging framed in the hall, and I cringe every time I see my llama face. I should've smiled."

Randi chuckles and turns her picture to face the wall. "I have an idea. Do you want to fly my kite in the backyard? I could sit outside for a little while if Mom says it's okay."

"If you feel up to it, you can go out—if you bundle up." Mrs. Picconi's arches her eyebrows and looks unsure.

"That would be fun." I'm grinning ear to ear.

Outside, the blustery wind makes it seem like a different day from this morning when I was raking with Dad. I run around in circles, lifting the dragon kite to the wind. It looks like the picture of one we saw in class when we learned about Chinese culture. They have a festival in China where kids fly kites and let them go soaring into the sky to take away any sadness, bad luck, and sickness. Do they believe cancer can fly away? How do they explain sickness coming back? Maybe they think the kite didn't go high enough. Maybe it got stuck in a tree and fell back to the ground.

Randi reclines on the lounge chair, shading her eyes from the late afternoon sun. I stand next to her, holding the kite string as the dragon ascends high above the trees. I'm tempted to try the superstition and let the kite go.

As I glance at Randi staring into the sky, I see the other Randi, the one who enjoys life. Her cheeks are rosy, and her expression is light and carefree. *Is she healthy?* She looks better than when she was cooped up inside. "You look pretty."

She smiles. "You need glasses."

Maybe she just needed sunlight to make her well again, like a touch of God's power. Doctors can be wrong. I don't think a kite can take her illness away, but I'm sure God can. She must be getting better!

"Hey!" Michael pops up from behind the bushes, and showers us with handfuls of leaves. "You little stinker!" Randi waves a finger at him and laughs.

"I'll get him!" After handing Randi the kite handle, I scoop up some leaves and chase Michael all over the backyard until I trap him by where the fence meets the bushes. "Here you go!" Michael dives on the ground as if shot by a bullet when the leaves shower him. Randi giggles at the whole scene.

"Ahh, it feels so good to be outside." Randi takes a deep breath of the cool air and sighs. "Look, there's Mom, peeking out the window—probably checking on me. She must think I'm still four years old."

I sit down next to Randi and relax with her while Michael circles the yard with the kite.

"Doesn't Michael look cute? Like Piglet being carried by the wind in *Winnie the Pooh*."

Randi doesn't answer. Her eyes are closed and her mouth is open. She's sound asleep. What should I do? Should I wake her up, or leave without saying anything, or go tell her mom she fell asleep? I wish this wouldn't keep happening.

Mrs. Picconi opens the sliding door. "Everything alright? Do you kids want a drink or snack?"

"No thanks," I answer. "Randi fell asleep a little while ago. I should probably go home now."

Mrs. Picconi nods. "By the way, thank you for raking the lawn. And thank your father for me too. Usually Mr. Picconi … well, he hasn't been himself lately. None of us have." Mrs. Picconi adjusts the cushion next to Randi's tilted head. "Sometimes it's hard to ask for help. Anyway, that was kind of you."

I can feel my face turning red. Again.

"You're welcome. We were out there anyway." I hope that didn't sound stupid.

"You know … " Mrs. Picconi is next to me now. She takes my hand and squeezes it gently. "Randi has been noticeably happier since you've been coming over. Even Miss Barbara has said so a number of times. You're a good friend to her."

"Thanks. I had fun here today." Now I'm ripe strawberry red. Why does the color of my face change so easily? I wish my skin was darker so my emotions wouldn't come bursting through my cheeks.

I walk home questioning myself. *I had fun here today*. Why did I put it that way? Maybe it sounds like I don't usually have fun there. I could have said something about Randi being a good friend to me, or how much I like her, or something else.

The wind has deposited some new leaves to replace the ones we raked. Removing every leaf from where it doesn't belong seems an impossible task. Is that what cancer is like to Randi? Just when it starts to look like the cancer is gone, more cancer blows in to take its place.

Isabelle's Cadillac drives by. I'm so deep in thought I barely notice. I look at my watch. They're probably returning from the roller rink. Even though it's Saturday, skating day, the day I used to live for, I haven't thought about Great Skates until right now. It's not important anymore. How was I able to have fun skating before, knowing that Randi was in and out of the hospital?

I close my front door and look out the window. Strong winds blow the rain diagonally. I'm glad we raked earlier today. Tomorrow there will surely be lots of wiggly creatures hiding in the leaves. In spite of the rain, I feel happy. Maybe Randi's getting better. Maybe my life is getting better too.

33

Mrs. Picconi holds the door open. "Hey, you're back. Did you have a nice time? "

"Yes, I loved skiing."

"Randi's just waking up from a nap. I know she'll be happy to see you."

I smile and run up the steps to her bedroom as I have so many times before, but not so many since our second chance at friendship. Climbing up these steps feels like visiting my kindergarten classroom, familiar and foreign. I'm climbing the past, a time that seems so long ago, a happy time when the worst challenge Randi and I faced was coloring within the lines.

Randi's steps aren't the same. The closer they lead me to past memories, the sadder I feel.

"Hey, how was your trip?" asks Randi.

"Great!" I try to ignore the memories of her room that flash in front of me as I rock in her rocking chair. Randi's room doesn't smell like baby powder anymore. It smells more like medicine, sterile plastic, and food trays. Her bedroom has become a hospital room, not a—

Randi interrupts my thoughts. "Tell me what you did there."

"We stayed at a family resort with lots of kids and went downhill skiing. Looking down the hills was scary the first time, but it was more fun than riding roller coasters." *Is Randi getting upset hearing about all the fun I had?*

"I'd love to try skiing some day."

"I wish you could have come with us. Maybe next year …" I let that idea drift off.

"Did Laurie and your parents ski?"

"Laurie did, kind of. She had some trouble getting up the mountain and down. The t-bar dragged her to the mountaintop on her belly, and she slid down the steep and bumpy slope on her butt. Good thing she wore puffy snow pants."

Randi laughs when I act out the scene.

"Last night they had the best New Year's Eve party and I—" Randi's stops laughing, so I stop.

"I wish I went to a party. My dad stayed out all night and Mom was …" She shakes her head. "Oh, forget it. Let's go watch TV or something."

We head downstairs to sit by her fireplace. Randi pulls open the curtains and shouts, "Wow! Come and see this."

I press my nose against the glass like Randi. "Wow! It's beautiful." A foot of snow blankets her backyard. The snow hushes even the slightest movement of the trees and clouds the view of neighboring houses. Gentle flurries persist, painting the picnic table a brilliant white.

"Imagine this is the castle tower, high in a white cloud." Randi slides open the door to reach her hand out and catch some of the melting flakes. "And these are magical flakes to grant wishes." I join her and yank my hand in to see what I caught. For a second, I see the crystal shapes before they melt into a shapeless water droplet. We taste our wet fingers, close our eyes, and wish.

When I open my eyes, Randi pulls out a game from her coffee table. "Do you want to play Boggle? I play against Miss Barbara every day, and she hasn't beaten me yet. I'm training to be the first Boggle Champion in the next Olympics." Randi chuckles.

I smile, but my mind gets tangled on her words. The next Olympics is four years away. Will she be here then?

We sink into the couch and turn the hourglass-shaped timer to begin. A few sounds disturb the silence: embers crackle in the fireplace, pencils scratch paper, and dice clink in a cup and clatter onto the table. I'm sure the sand piles at the bottom faster than a minute. I have the urge to flip it over, just to give myself more time. Too late. The snowstorm within the hourglass reaches its peak. I'd like to smash this rotten piece of plastic that has the power to end the game.

"Remember when we made that huge snowman on my front lawn?" Randi asks as we add up our points.

"Yeah. Your mom found an old hat and scarf, and your dad put a pair of goofy glasses on the snowman's bumpy head—glasses with a plastic nose attached. It was so cold that the snowman didn't melt for weeks!"

"It could have lasted until spring if Justin and his friends didn't karate chop it to death."

"Remember—we got so mad at them, and had a mean snowball fight, boys against girls."

"They threw icy snowballs that felt like baseballs."

"The boys were definitely showing off."

Randi flattens her cheek against the frosty glass. "Look! It's coming down harder now."

"Too bad the snow didn't fall last week, in time for Christmas." In my silly mood, I sing, "I was dreaming of a white Christmas, the hmm…hmm…I used to know." I always forget the words to Christmas carols.

"I never could understand that song. We don't have any Chanukah songs about having a white Chanukah. And I don't know why we sing a song about dreidels."

"Yeah, I don't know why we sing about flying reindeers and a fat man in a red suit sliding down chimneys. I used to wonder why he didn't fly his sleigh over to your house. Why wouldn't he fill stockings in Jewish homes?"

"I wondered that too."

Mom and Dad explained that Santa could only land on homes with Christmas lights outside to guide his sleigh. Even a four-year-old wouldn't believe that reason!"

"I used to feel bad that you had only one day to open presents and that was it," admits Randi. "And I liked being able to celebrate both holidays. My dad taught us Christmas is when Jesus was born, and my mom taught us the meaning of Chanukah and lighting the candles. She wanted us to grow up following the Jewish traditions."

Randi wins the first game.

"I guess you *are* a champion." I'm not surprised she won. My mind was doing mental gymnastics, since she got me thinking of heaven.

Just as we turn the hourglass over for another game, Michael comes inside, stomping his boots. He leaps in the room and places his cold, red hands on Randi's cheeks. "Ah! You're freezing!" screams Randi.

Michael gives her a bear hug. "I know. Want to feel how cold again?"

"No!"

As he sits down to play with us, I stare at him, thinking how cute he looks with rosy cheeks, puppy dog eyes, and pin-straight, dark hair like his father's. Randi used to look more like her mom with her lighter, wavy hair, but now her short, dark hair looks more like Michael's. Michael seems taller and thinner today, especially standing next to Randi, whose face reminds me of a pudgy baby's.

What is his life like right now? He has so much more to worry about than most kids his age. I'm not sure if it is because he is a couple years older now or that he grew up quicker dealing with Randi's sickness, but he doesn't seem like a little brother anymore.

Randi has also changed in the last couple of months as our friendship is returning to what it was. *Would Randi call me her friend now?* I hope so. I thought she couldn't forgive me and would stay distant, but most of the time, she is as she was—sweet, cheerful, and friendly. Sometimes I forget how sick she is. Other times I can't get the word cancer out of my head, and have to pretend something blew in my eyes. Sometimes I wonder how Randi feels. I'm mad and sad at that one word that has the power to end her life—cancer—the sand in the hourglass. But God could flip it over.

Michael looks up at the clock on the wall. "Let's watch the Muppets. It's on now."

"Okay, put it on." Randi looks over to me, "Can you stay long enough to watch it?"

"Sure, I'm supposed to get home by six for dinner. That's enough time."

The Muppet Show is another one of those kid's programs I just don't get, but everyone else seems to think is hilarious. I laugh along anyway.

"Kuh-*rum*-bah!" screams Miss Piggy as she karate chops Kermit the Frog.

"Kuh-*rum*-bah!" Michael imitates her in a squeaky voice and karate chops the air.

I laugh because they do, but I can't stand Miss Piggy. Her high-pitched voice is almost as bad as the broken jack-in-the-box that Laurie still has in her room. Jack screams in pain when he jumps out. My ears ring when I hear either one of them.

The door that leads from the den to the garage screeches open. The screech echoes Miss Piggy's voice. Mr. Picconi trudges in, stomping his boots on the mat.

"Hey, my fav'rit show is on. Howz Kermit doin'?" He gives Michael a high five, stumbles around the reclining chair, and gives me a high-ten. Then he kisses Randi's forehead tenderly.

"Hi, Dad." Randi smiles a concerned smile. "Where were you?"

"Oh, jus' buildin' a rocket in the garage, nothin' too interestin'."

Did Randi and Michael think their dad sounded different? I would never ask, but I think he's drunk. Maybe Randi did notice. She bites her lip and stares directly at the screen. I pretend I don't notice anything unusual and listen to annoying Miss Piggy.

Is Randi angry? She doesn't have eyebrows, making it hard to read her facial expressions.

I relax when she asks, "Do they have to show a summer episode in January? They dance around in Hawaiian shirts and hula skirts while we're trapped inside."

"I was thinking the same thing!" My mind wanders. Could we also feel the same feelings at the same time? Could we have an itch in the same spot? Will we have to sneeze at the same time? What would it be like if we could trade feelings, and I could feel what it is like to have cancer? Randi could feel what it's like to be healthy again.

The clock chimes six and interrupts my daydream. It's time to go home.

The walk home through the falling snow reminds me that vacation is over, unless the snow gets heavy enough to cancel classes. I hope so. I'm not ready to deal with more miserable days at school—and there's still over half a year of them left.

34

After slamming down on the snooze button for the third time, I leap out of bed and rush over to the window. All I see is white—much more than yesterday—and snow is still falling! Mom knocks and steps into my room.

"You can go back to bed. School is closed."

My wish is granted! I jump back into bed, pull the blanket over my head to block the light and trap my warm breath and dreams.

I can't sleep. Every time a snowplow roars by, I wake in a panic, thinking I just missed the bus. It takes a few minutes for my heart to stop racing. *Oh no, I'm late, I'm late.* I'm the rabbit racing through Wonderland to catch the bus ... slam the snooze button. Beep, beep. *Oh no, I'm ...* slam the snooze button. Enough of this stupid routine. Time to get up and enjoy the snow and one more day of vacation.

Looking out at the driveway, I remember the downside to snowstorms—shoveling. This time, however, Laurie and I get out early and clear the driveway. We shovel around the parked squash-mobile and smile at each other. Dad's home today. That means sledding.

"Wow! I'm in shock." Dad holds his face, in disbelief, mouth open. "You girls woke up and shoveled without being told?"

"Yep."

"Well, how would you like to go sledding at the golf course when you finish?"

Laurie bursts out in excitement, "Yes! Look how much we shoveled already. We're almost done. Can I ask Justin if he wants to come with us?"

"Sure. We have some extra sleds." Dad turns to me. "Do you want to invite a friend too?"

"I would, but Randi can't, and I don't want to ask anyone else."

After piling on so many clothes, I can barely bend and feel like an unattractive stuffed potato. I need air! I rush outside to help put the sleds in the car. Michael and his dad are building a snowman on their front lawn. As I wave to them, Randi waves back from her dining room window. She is watching them. I smile, but I wonder if I should have invited her, even though I know what the answer would be.

Thank God we're at the golf course and can tumble out of the car. Three kids stuffed in puffy coats and snow-pants, buried under sleds, do not make a comfortable ride. I think I'm going to scream if I can't get to an unreachable itch I have on my back under my layers. And I'm stuck—pinned under piles of snow gear. "Get me out of here!"

"Hold on. I'm coming." Dad lifts the sleds off me and helps us slide out of the car.

I charge up the slippery hill. The scent of a distant fireplace drifts across the golf course. With the sun reflecting off the snow, the ground and sky blend together into a wall of white light, but the trees cast purple shadows to show where they divide. Yesterday's problems fade into tomorrow. Today's for flying. Downhill, snow-drenched, sub-zero flying.

Laurie tries to climb and carry her sled, but the icy snow is too slippery for her.

"Help!" Laurie yells as she falls onto her smooth plastic sled—repeating her skiing trouble—and slides backward to the bottom of the hill, right in the path of some kids coming down. I close my eyes. Yep, they all crash into Laurie. Amazingly, no one is hurt, but my stomach hurts from laughing so hard.

"Are you okay down there?" I call. She looks helpless in the snow, so I climb down to her.

"My face is cold."

"Here, come this way. It's less steep." I take off my bulky scarf and wrap it around her neck and chin to warm her wet cheeks.

"Thanks." At the top she catches up to Justin.

Watching Laurie sledding with Justin, laughing and being silly, I realize I am jealous—not of their friendship, but jealous of their *normal* friendship. I want to share this good time with Randi, but I can't.

Randi was here with us two years ago. Each hill we tried was a new experience. Some were bumpy and jostled us about, throwing us up in the air. Some were smooth and steep, sending us down at rocket speed. Some were gentle slopes, letting us coast for a breather. Some were treacherous if not ridden carefully. Our last ride down was one of those treacherous ones. Randi and I were together on Dad's old sled made of wood with red handles to steer. We picked up some good speed, but couldn't stop.

We fell off and rolled in the snow, seconds before the sled crashed into a massive tree at the edge of the woods. After coming that close to colliding, my parents decided it was time to go. They wanted to bring Randi home in one piece.

I want it to be *that* time again—minus the crash. The slopes haven't changed, but it isn't the same without her. It's not nearly as much fun.

"Ow! What was that?" I turn around to see Todd (of all people) taking aim with another snowball. Todd? It's hard to tell if it's him since he's wearing a hat and scarf, and my eyes are watery in the wind. *It has to be*—I recognize the blue and white striped Mets jacket. I've stared at that coat every day during gym class since Mr. Burke makes everyone brave the frigid temperatures for soccer.

For a few seconds, I stand there in shock until my senses kick in. I make a quick snowball to get him back. *Should I be mad at him? Did he throw it because he likes me, or was he teasing me because he thinks I'm a dork?* I want to hit him in the face with a snowball, so I throw a solid round one as hard as I can. It misses him by a few yards (no surprise) and lands on a bulky man who doesn't look too happy. "What the—!" the man yells.

Todd falls back in the snow hysterically laughing. I stomp back up the hill, embarrassed at my poor aiming skills and plot my snowy revenge.

I hop on the sled and aim it where Todd now stands with his back to me. I'm going fast—too fast. Uh oh. Just at the last second, he turns around as I try to tilt the sled away from him, but the handle catches his boot laces and knocks him off his feet. Todd lands on his face in the snow.

"Hey, come here!" he hollers, wiping snow off his mouth with his wool scarf.

Now I'm nervous. "Are you okay? I didn't mean to bump into you like that."

"You didn't? Sure you weren't trying to get me back for the snowball I whaled you with?"

"Well, maybe the thought did cross my mind." I'm in full blush now, especially on my cold nose. I probably look like Rudolph.

"Come with me." Todd grabs my hand and leads me back up the steep side. I love holding his hand, even through thick gloves. At the top, he sits down on his sled and pats the space behind him. "Hop on. We'll go even faster together, so hold on tight."

I'm like a pretzel wrapped around him. A toasty, warm pretzel. We zoom down at what feels like bobsled speed. I'm not as cold with his body blocking the wind. This is the best way to sled. I can't believe I'm holding on to Todd Williams!

"Watch out!" Todd shouts, but I don't know why. Then I do. We hit a bump and fly off, landing next to each other in the snow.

"That was fun!" I can feel my smiling lips cracking in the cold.

After zooming down together three more times, it's over. Dad is calling me to leave. Seems he's about to turn purple. I wave and wonder if Todd will be different to me at school.

This time I take off my coat and snow pants before smushing into the seat next to Laurie. I'm warm enough without feeling like a baked potato.

"That was fun. Let's come back tomorrow," Laurie says as she bounces up and down.

Justin leans over the front seat. "Thanks for taking me. I've never gone sledding before."

Dad ruffles his wet hair. "I'm glad you all had a good time," he adds, "and no broken bones."

As I contemplate Justin never going sledding before and stick my head out the open window for fresh air, I notice Todd helping some girl with curly blond hair climb up the hill. He's holding her hand. *Oh, my gosh! It's Julie.* She turns and winks at me. *Oh, I hate her smug face.*

Dad looks at me in the rear view mirror. "So who was the boy you were sledding with?"

"No one. Just some jerk from school."

"Oh? I thought you and the jerk were having a good time together."

"Well, I was at first. But I can't stand him." Dad doesn't press it.

At home, I slam the car door shut and glance over at the lonely snowman on Randi's lawn. He's wearing those same funny glasses. Randi rests at the window again. After dragging a sled to the garage, I trudge through the snow to go see her.

"Did you see the snowman Michael made for me? He said it was a gift since I couldn't build one. Isn't that thoughtful?"

"Yeah, Randi, he's real nice." *Nicer than me.*

Now I'm trying to hold back a stubborn tear that's determined to fall. It will be good to go to school. I won't have to look at that sad snowman.

***

This month, classes haven't been so bad. Teachers seem rested from the break, and today we celebrate Inauguration Day. It's a big deal at school. Ms. Sullivan decorated the room with red, white, and blue balloons. She passes out donuts and throws confetti and hope at us. She voted for Reagan and he won by a landslide. The donuts work. Our class is excited about politics for the first time.

Of course, Todd is chosen to walk around with the donut box. He brings them to me first. A peace offering maybe, but I won't look at him. I choose a glazed munchkin and stare at his eyes. Sky blue with dark edges. He winks. I bite my cheeks to stop smiling and fold the napkin over my munchkin.

"Yesterday, the same day President Reagan was sworn in, Iran released the fifty-two remaining American hostages. This is more than a coincidence." Ms. Sullivan bubbles with patriotism. "Reagan brings change and hope to America."

We clap with stuffed mouths. I leave class believing America's problems are over. I want to believe Randi's getting better too.

35

The paint in the can looks almost edible when I stir it, so smooth and creamy, like a milkshake. I don't know what flavor purple would be, grape or boysenberry maybe, but it's my favorite now. I am determined to surround myself in it. My parents wouldn't let me paint my ugly wallpaper, so I convinced Laurie to switch bedrooms with me. It wasn't hard to convince her since my room is bigger than hers. My plan is to redecorate and escape my prison of yellow flowers and orange grass-rug. Freedom at last!

Good thing it's warm enough to keep the window open and let out the fumes. Otherwise, Mom might find me passed out in the purple paint tray. Actually, I like the smell. Mixed with the fragrance of the lilac bushes outside, it's like painting spring in my room.

This whole renovation project began because of spring cleaning, another one of my most hated activities. At the sound of the first bird chirping, Mom decided we needed to clean our rooms, beginning with our closets. Once I removed the three-foot-high pile of junk, I didn't want to put anything back. I decided my room needed a whole new look. I'm almost thirteen, almost a teenager. And a teenager should have a cool room. So here I am, creating a purple paradise.

"Your room looks nice."

"Thanks, Laur."

"But I still like the yellow room better. There's more room for my toys."

"Well, I'm not finished yet. I need to hang some posters of cute boys from my *Teen* magazine." I show Laurie some of my favorite actors, but she is not impressed.

"Yuck! You should put up pictures of cute animals like I do."

"No thanks—hey, look at this model's hair. I'd love to have long, wavy hair like that."

"Yeah, me too."

"Maybe I can convince Mom and Dad to let me get a perm like some girls in school have."

"I want one too."

"Well, I'll ask at dinnertime when they're in a good mood—after I get home from Randi's. I need a break from decorating."

Just as I am about to knock on Randi's front door, Mrs. Grayson, my fifth-grade teacher comes out. I must look like I'm staring at a ghost. I was definitely not expecting her to open the door. She is lugging an oversized book bag in one hand and juggling more books in the other. I hold the door for her, smiling like a ripe tomato, and not knowing what to say, as usual.

"Well, hello there, Francie. How's seventh grade going?"
She remembered my name?

"Okay. My grades are good, but it's definitely a lot harder."

"I'm not surprised you're doing well. You were always a good student in my class."

I'm relieved that she didn't bring up the giggling fits I used to have while sitting next to Nina. "Thanks. Are you Randi's tutor?" *Well, that was a stupid question—of course she is.*

"Yes, I have been for about a year now. Usually, I leave by twelve o'clock, but today we started late. That's why you haven't seen me before today," she explains. "Randi talks about you a lot. I remember when you first told me about her. You're both special girls. Well, I better get going. It was nice to see you."

"I didn't know Mrs. Grayson is your tutor."

"I thought … I … told you." Randi's eyelids droop as she talks to me in slow motion.

"She was one of my favorite teachers. How do you like her?"

No answer.

"Randi! I asked how you like her." I'm practically screaming. Mrs. Picconi told me that Randi was having trouble hearing lately.

214

Miss Barbara's heavy footsteps make me turn my head. "She's exhausted today. She could hardly keep her eyes open during her lessons." Miss Barbara walks me to the door, squeezing my hand. "Here. Randi wanted to give this to you."

"Thanks." I open the card she hands me. It's an invitation to Randi's twelfth birthday party at the Ground Round next week. I'm surprised again. I didn't think Randi would have a party. I wonder if she asked for it, if she knows. On the way back home, I try to come up with a good present to get her, something special.

Back in my freshly painted purple room, I begin my magazine search for the best-looking movie stars to adorn my walls. I find a nice Michael Jackson poster and a Ralph Maccheo page. I hope doing this cheers me up. There's nothing more disappointing than wanting to visit my friend and being sent home because she fell asleep. Again.

As I flip through the pages and search for the picture of the model with the gorgeous, wavy hair, Laurie walks in.

"Here it is. I'll show Mom and Dad this picture to explain how we want our hair styled." I hold the magazine open for Laurie to look.

"I like it. You could bring it now. Dinner's ready. Mom sent me to get you."

"Okay, here I go. Cross your fingers. What did she make for dinner anyway?"

"Pepper steak and rice."

"UGH! I thought that's what I smelled, but I won't complain. I don't want to ruin our chance for getting perms."

Before I even put one forkful in my mouth, Laurie bursts out with our idea. "We want to get our hair wavy like all the other girls in school!"

So much for easing into the conversation gracefully. I put my fork down.

"Can we get perms? All the girls at school are doing it, and it will help us get ready faster in the morning. Please?" With Mom's eyes on me, I force a tiny chunk of steak down my throat.

Mom raises her eyebrows and looks at Dad. He's chewing. We look at both of them, pleading with puppy dog eyes. Dad swallows. "Your mother and I will discuss it after dinner, but I happen to think a neat, chin-length haircut would be classier."

"Yuck! We'd look like boys." I hold my hair up and scrunch my nose for a demonstration. "See."

Mom hands me a roll. "Finish your dinner now, and we'll talk about it later."

"Oh, my gosh! That pepper-steak seemed to be growing. I didn't think I'd *ever* finish," I complain to Laurie. We sit on the couch and pretend to watch TV. I don't think we look convincing though, sitting in front of the news listening to

President Reagan talk about the Evil Empire. We strain to hear the muffled conversation going on behind Mom and Dad's bedroom door. Our eyes grow wide as they come out with the decision. I imagine a drum roll.

Dad is the first to speak. "Okay girls, we decided that since you both had good grades on your first three report cards, you can get perms to celebrate. Just promise to keep up the good work until the end of the school year."

"I'll make an appointment in a few weeks." Mom grins. Michael's Hair Salon is one of her favorite places. I'm sure she can relate to our excitement.

"Yeah! Thanks! In a few weeks we'll look like movie stars." Laurie and I dance around, celebrating.

Dad joins in and spins us around. "Would it be all right for me to shut off the TV now, or do you still want to watch *World News Tonight*?"

"I think we saw enough. We got the news we wanted— new hair styles!" Thinking of news, I remember my invitation. "Oh, I almost forgot. I got an invitation to Randi's birthday party at the Ground Round next Saturday with her family. Can I go?"

"Sure, you can go. We don't have any plans next weekend," says Mom. "Do you know what you'd like to get her?"

"I'm not sure, but something special and I'll do a drawing for her also."

"Good idea. We can shop after school tomorrow."

It's refreshing to open the door to my new room, crash on the bed, and soak up the purpleness. I'm inspired to make a homemade card for Randi. After hunting for a good picture to copy, I find a sweet photo of a young girl swinging on a tire hanging from a tree. It's perfect.

For the rest of the evening, I work on the drawing for Randi until I'm pleased with it. Hours have disappeared. I can't believe how late it is.

I try to fall asleep for what feels like forever. My mind keeps racing, thinking about what I should get for Randi—something she'd love, something that shows her how much she means to me. Though I'm half-awake, an idea comes to me. Randi once told me she wanted to write about her experience with cancer. I can get her a journal. I picture Randi sitting at her desk and pouring her heart onto the pages as I slip into a dream ... Randi reads it to her children, a boy and a girl identical to her and Michael. They sit with legs folded. They listen and wait—wait to see what will happen on the next page.

36

I'm ready to go to Randi's party. Then I wonder. *What if I have nothing to say?* Maybe I'm not ready. My lips could freeze shut like ice does to the car door after a storm. I have reason to fear this since it's happened before. Nothing's worse than feeling like a blank piece of paper—so blank there aren't even blue lines running across.

So I think about her presents. A rose-colored journal, decorated with white flowers and a statue of two girls sitting on a bench eating ice cream cones with the words *Friends Forever* written on it. Mom placed them together in one box and wrapped it beautifully with ribbons and shiny silver paper. I may not have anything important to say, but I have the perfect gift that looks ready for royalty.

"Come on in," says Mrs. Picconi. "We'll be leaving for the restaurant in a few minutes. Oh, how beautiful! It'll be a shame to tear it open."

I smile.

"You can give it to Randi before we leave, if you'd like."

Randi is sitting in the den. I rush over to her.

First Randi calls her parents over to look at the card. I'm embarrassed and proud at the same time as they ooh and ah over my homemade creation. She attempts to open the present, painstakingly slow, as if it were wrapped with crazy glue instead of tape.

"Francie, can you help me? I'm a little tired."

"Sure." In a second it's open, but I'm not as excited anymore. I hate seeing Randi look so weak.

"Oh! A journal. It's perfect to write my story in." She pulls out the statue from the tissue paper. "This is beautiful. I love it! You'll always be my best friend." Randi leans over to hug me. I don't say anything back. The stupid lump is back again and I'm strangling on it.

Randi has an even harder time going to her party than opening the present. She struggles to walk to the car. She is out of breath walking up the few steps to the restaurant, but refuses her father's offer to help. Even worse, she dozes off while eating her meal. This is not the celebration I expected. The food is good, but I hardly taste it. Watching Randi sleep has my mind racing at full speed. I'm not a blank piece of paper anymore. I'm a sheet with a thousand words with scribbles and doodles all along the edges, making it more difficult to open my mouth and talk than I imagined. If only my life were a story on paper, I could tear it into a million pieces and start over.

Mr. Picconi watches Randi too, and drinks wine—too much wine. He jokes with the waitress. "Where's the cake? We'd like to sing for this year's birthday, not next year's!"

Mrs. Picconi nudges him. "That's enough," she whispers through clenched teeth.

Randi opens her eyes. They're swimming with tears. "Just stop it! I can't take this anymore. Your stupid drinks are ruining our family. You pass out, Mom cries, Michael cries, and I'm still sick. Why are you doing this to yourself? To us? We need a dad."

The party is silent.

Mr. Picconi pushes back his chair and mumbles something. It sounded like "sorry pumpkin," but I'm not sure what he said. He heads for the restroom.

I trace the checkerboard pattern on my plate with a French fry. Randi's cousins are twirling their ice cubes with a straw. I'm relieved when the waitress arrives with the cake, and we sing "Happy Birthday."

As our table bursts out in song, people at another table stare and whisper. Are they interested in a birthday party, or are they wondering why a young girl looks the way she does? Though I can't read their minds, I am angry with these nosey neighbors. I imagine them making fun of this overweight girl with a crew cut whose dad is too loud.

After the cake, we play some of the arcade games. Randi climbs into the mini-corvette seat and calls me over. I plop down next to her, and we race the Indy 500. Randi is lively again, shouting "Go! Go!" at the screen as she tries to win the race. It almost makes up for the awkward dinner.

"Watch out! I'm catching up to you," shouts Randi.

"No, you won't. I've got one more lap." I want Randi to win though. "Hey! You knocked me off the road! No fair!"

"See—I told you I'd catch up!" Randi giggles.

Mr. Picconi reappears and stands behind us, watching. When the game stops, he leans over the seat and says something to Randi. She glances my way. "I'll be right back." She gets up and follows him outside. I keep playing, but it's hard to drive when I can see them hug through the window. Mrs. Picconi and Michael join them in their hug like a football huddle. I smash my car into a field of cows and lose the game.

As we gather up our party bags filled with lollipops, a yo-yo, and a rope bracelet, a girl about Randi's age from the whispering table approaches us and hands Randi a miniature stuffed polar bear wearing a birthday sash.

"Here … happy birthday. I won it at the arcade games, but I thought I'd give it to you since it's your birthday."

"Thank you. That's so nice of you."

I'm glad I was wrong. I guess I've become Randi's guard dog. If anyone dares to make one wrong move—a curious stare, a nasty comment—I want to attack. It's a good thing I didn't bite this time.

"Did you have a good time?" Mom opens my goody bag.

"It was okay. I liked playing the arcade games. The cake was too sweet, but I liked my hamburger. Mr. Picconi drank too much wine. Mrs. Picconi and Randi got mad at him, but they worked it out. It was just uncomfortable."

"Oh, that's too bad. Mr. Picconi is going through a rough time. He needs our prayers too."

I nod, but I doubt prayers will help him, especially mine. I prayed that God would make Randi get better. But she's worse. I prayed that he would give her another friend, but she's still stuck with me. What will happen if I pray for Mr. Picconi? My prayers are more like a curse.

37

"Francie, wake up! Do you know what day it is?" I roll over and crack my eyes open. My sister's head blocks the glaring sunrise coming in the window. "It's Friday. That means our hair appointment is just one day away. Can you believe it?"

"Uh huh. Good night. It's too early." I pull my quilt over my head.

Every day after school I get to hear Laurie's countdown. It started the first day of June: twelve days to our perms ... twelve ... eleven days ... ten ... and so on. We're getting closer to blast off.

Yesterday I told Randi that I was getting a perm, but no one else knows. I'd rather surprise everyone at school with my new look. Although most kids there probably don't care what my hair looks like, someone may notice. If it comes out nice, I'll enter one of those modeling contests in the magazine.

I can't concentrate on my schoolwork today. I keep thinking about my hair appointment and looking around to see which girls have perms. I've counted eleven who I am sure used to have straight hair.

***

Finally Saturday. Laurie forgot to say blast off.

Laurie and I are escorted to our side-by-side chairs where Kathy and Linda, our chic stylists, begin rolling our hair and pinning it. We scrunch our faces and laugh at how silly we look. Magazines help pass the time, but it takes more time than we can handle sitting in one spot. Mom did warn us. We thought she was kidding when she told us she was going home and would come back later. Wow! She definitely made the right decision.

Next, we have to sit under hair dryers like Wilma and Betty from the Flintstones cartoon. At least our dryers aren't made out of stone. Across from us sit two old ladies who must be regulars. They call the hairdresser over and tell her the time is up. The hairdresser agrees.

"I don't want it as tight as it came out last week," whines the one with the bluish hair.

I can't imagine doing this every week. You have to be at least eighty to think this is a rockin' time. I am about to scream and run out of here—just give up on the whole curly hair idea—if I have to sit any longer. This better be worth it.

I'm starting to worry that I might look like a poodle or like that old lady. I'll have to lock myself in my room until it grows out.

"Laurie, are you awake?" I guess not. My eyes keep shutting too. The constant humming of the dryers could put anyone to sleep. Waiting and waiting for the timer…

Dinggggg. Kathy comes over and lifts the dryer off. "Are you ready for the grand finale?"

"Definitely!"

"Well, let's go!" My scalp tingles as she unwinds the curling rods to reveal shoulder-length strands of spirals. I'm fascinated. I've never had the slightest bend to my hair. At the same time, Linda unrolls Laurie's hair. She looks amazing.

My hair looks so full. Is it too full? Do I look like I stuck my finger in a socket? I hope that's not what kids at school will say. I hope Todd likes curls. My hair feels soft and bouncy, but it is such a change. I can't decide if I like it or not. One thing's for sure—I will tell my parents I love it.

"Do you love it?" Kathy asks with a beaming smile as if reading my mind. "You look awesome! You must have a terrific hairstylist."

Right on cue, Mom walks in. I can see her through the mirror, paying the cashier. As she walks toward us, I watch her, anticipating her reaction.

"You both look beautiful." Judging by Mom's facial expression, however, I'm not sure I believe her. She is half-smiling, phony, and not like herself at all. Now I'm worried.

Is she going to tell us the truth in the car? Will she say we look awful and it was a waste of money? Actually, that's more Dad's style. Mom would say it in a softer way, like "You look pretty, but your straight hair was nice too."

Laurie and I sit down in the backseat. Mom gets in and slams the front door. She must hate our perms. She hasn't said a word since we walked out of the salon and hasn't even started up the car. Mom's eyes stare at us through the rearview mirror.

"Girls, I need to tell you something. Some bad news . . ." Mom begins, but pauses to take a breath. My heart is pounding out of my chest. "Oh, this is so hard." Mom turns around to face us. "This morning ... Randi went into a coma."

I'm not sure I know what happens in a coma, and I'm sure Laurie doesn't know. But the tone of Mom's voice tells me it's serious—just like when I first heard she had cancer.

Laurie starts crying. "Does that mean she died?"

"No, it means she is in a deep sleeping state and can't wake up."

I am not crying, just in shock. "How long will she stay like that? Can she get out of a coma?"

"I don't know. No one does. She could come out of it, but she might not."

"So where is she?"

"She was in her bed when I left, but is probably at the hospital by now. She never woke up today." Mom wipes her eyes, starts the engine, and we drive toward home. In the rearview mirror, her cheeks look wet with tears. I should be crying by now too, but I can't. I picture Randi lying on her pink bed, sleeping heavily. Any minute now, she will wake up. She has to.

The ride home is painfully slow—as if the car is standing still. But even without moving, we arrive. Before I can get out of the back seat, I hear a strange noise, like a screeching bird. "What is that sound?"

I open the car door. Now I hear it clearly—someone screaming.

It's Michael. He runs around the bushes between our houses and charges toward us, yelling at the top of his lungs. When he reaches the driveway, he collapses with his face in the grass, kicking and punching the ground with all his might. The screeching continues. I cover my ears. Mom rushes over to him.

"What's wrong? Are you okay? Tell me." Mom grabs him in her arms and holds him tightly.

"She's dead! Randi is dead," Michael gasps between crying spasms. Mom hugs him and rocks as she'd comfort an infant.

I can't move my feet. I watch, mesmerized, as if I am watching a movie—a tearjerker. This isn't real. Randi can't be dead. I was over there yesterday. She was alive. We celebrated her birthday just last month. We celebrated her life.

I close my burning eyes. The salt stings and the lump in my throat is the size of a tennis ball. I don't know what to do, so I run to my room.

Laurie is already sobbing in her room. I didn't see her disappear. She must have run in right after hearing those horrible words: "She's dead." I hear them over and over again and again. I cover my head with my pillow and weep.

38

Mom rubs my back and offers to cook me some food. Though eating is the last thing on my mind, I desperately need some water to quench the fire in my throat. I must have fallen asleep.

I start to get up. Big mistake. My head pounds. The room spins like I'm floating in a purple sky. After regaining my balance, I stumble by my mirror, stunned at the image before me. I already forgot about my long-awaited perm, which now looks like a tangled mess inviting some bird to land in it. A wavy imprint of my ruffled bedspread runs across my cheek like a scar. Swollen red eyes stare back at me. This is not the new look I imagined. In the mirror, I see Dad standing in my doorway.

"Hi." I'm afraid he'll tell me how bad my hair looks, but he just hugs me. There is nothing to say.

I'm glad I can't see into the Picconi's house. Every room must reek of sadness. In our house, the mirrors are a problem for me. Every time I see my new hair, I see death. I'm angry I had it done. I never want to go back to that salon again. I'll always remember that parking lot—where I heard about Randi's coma, her last step before she died.

Mom warns me. "You should go in the other room while I make some phone calls. I told Mrs. Picconi I'd let the neighbors know Randi's funeral service is tomorrow. I also said I'd call their friends who've moved away. I hate calling with such awful news."

This is moving too fast. I'm not ready to go to her funeral this soon. I've been to one other funeral—my grandfather's—but that was a few years ago, and he was Catholic. I don't know what a Jewish service will be like. I hope there isn't an open casket. I couldn't handle that.

All night I had crazy dreams about the funeral. In one, I got lost and didn't get there in time. I let her down. She wanted me there, where she could talk to me, but I missed my chance. In the dream, my parents didn't want me to go to the funeral. But it's the day, and I know I have to be there.

After brushing my teeth, I rummage through my closet, a forest of spring colors. Half the clothes I've outgrown. Mom suggests wearing the navy blue dress I wore for Easter, except with a blue sweater instead of the white one it came with. Good enough.

I'll definitely need a sweater since it feels chilly for mid-May. It's overcast with bulging grey clouds. Maybe it was going to be sunny and warm, but God changed the weather with the news of Randi. It's like all the angels in heaven are crying and the sky has collected their tears.

Laurie cries on the way to the temple. But I don't. I think about death and heaven. Do people age there? Will she always look twelve?

My eyes fixate on the trees passing by at thirty miles per hour. Poplars, elms, oaks—they are traveling to a gathering in the forest. We are parked in the car—not driving to a horrible funeral. Bent trees, proud trees, dancing trees, twisted trees, even diseased trees. I'd rather think about maples than seeing Mr. and Mrs. Picconi. And Michael.

In a last minute panic, I blurt out, "What do I say to her parents?" I can't even utter the name Randi.

"You can say you are sorry," Dad says as he pulls into a parking spot. We all get out, pop up our umbrellas, and walk across a garden full of flowers and stones to enter the temple's side door. It would be beautiful if it weren't pouring rain. *Does it always rain for funerals?*

Right away, Mrs. Picconi sees me and hugs me. My throat tightens as I manage to say, "I'm so sorry."

"I know. You meant so much to Randi."

My eyes fill up with tears at the sound of her name, and my heart is filling up with guilt. The words Dad told me to say are true. I *am* sorry.

I am sorry for being a horrible friend when she needed me most.

I am sorry for being selfish, making excuses, and telling lies.

I am sorry for passing by Randi's house every day and not stopping.

I am sorry for pretending she wasn't there.

I am sorry Randi had to suffer alone and be sad at the end of her life.

I am sorry that I can never change what I did.

I am sorry that I can never get that time back.

I must be a symbol of Randi's pain to her parents. They must hate me. I hate myself right now. I don't deserve to sit near her family. We sit in the back row—my choice.

There are so many people here—so many I don't know. Some look like they might be from the high school—coworkers of Mrs. Picconi. Some used to be in Randi's class, like Kimmy. I also see a few teachers. One of them is Mrs. Grayson. It must be extra sad for her. Mr. and Mrs. Torelli, Isabelle, and Joey are here. They sit in the same row as Becky and her parents. Even Jake and Todd are here. Every seat is taken.

The service starts. I didn't think I was going to cry, but I am. I can hardly pay attention. My eyes keep moving to the casket. The lid is down. I can't believe Randi is lying inside that fancy grey box. Maybe that's why some people do open caskets—to prove the person, the body, is actually inside.

The rabbi speaks, but not for long. Mr. Picconi gets up to say something. This is the first time I've ever seen a completely serious Mr. Picconi. He talks about Randi's birth and how she grew up to be the ideal daughter.

"I knew she was strong from the first time she gripped my finger and batted her baby lashes. She was becoming quite the little gymnast as she got older, but her real strength was in her character. She was honest and kind and a fighter until the end. Even when she couldn't go to school anymore, she worked hard to earn straight A's. When Randi was in the hospital, she encouraged the other children and tried to make them laugh. I wonder where she got her silly side from?" He stops while a few people chuckle at his little joke. Then he dabs his eyes with a tissue.

"Her strength was definitely from her mom. Randi battled me to quit drinking. She had the wisdom to tell me that destroying myself wasn't going to save her, but would destroy our family instead. Even in her pain, she could see my anguish. Her sad eyes made me want to quit. She never gave up hope for me, even though I lost hope for her.

"I'm so sorry, Randi. I shouldn't make excuses, but I couldn't stand to watch you suffer, and watch you slowly die. I just wanted to pretend it wasn't happening." He sniffles and coughs back his tears. "Randi, for you I promise to stay sober. Randi, you were a beautiful jewel. We are going to miss you forever. We love you."

Mr. Picconi places a flower on Randi's casket and breaks down. People fumble for tissues. Some just wipe their eyes with their coat sleeves.

The rabbi introduces Michael. He wants to share some stories about Randi. I am trying hard to focus my glassy eyes on him.

"My sister was the best! She wasn't like most girls. She didn't play with dolls and stuff like that. She liked baseball and climbing trees. She even liked playing with matchbox cars. She was smart and funny. I wish she was still here. I am going to miss her so much!"

He breaks down too and walks off crying. Everyone around me is wiping away tears. This is the saddest day ever.

"Come and sign your name in the guest book." Dad guides me to a small table decorated with a candle and a pink bouquet.

The pen shakes in my fingers, making it hard to write neatly. While I struggle to write, the gentle weight of a hand presses my shoulders. Assuming it's Dad again, I turn around. But it's Mrs. Grayson. "I'm sorry," she says. "You must miss her."

The dam breaks and I can't control my grief. I weep and wail in outbursts that surprise me. The last time I saw Mrs. Grayson was at Randi's house. Randi and I were best friends. She doesn't know about that in-between time when I abandoned Randi, the time I am so ashamed of. Seeing Mrs. Grayson reminds me of the time before cancer came and changed everything. People keep trying to console me, making it worse. I can feel others staring at me as they walk by; even Jake and Todd see me. I can't stop sobbing, but I don't care.

Miss Barbara, Randi's nurse, comes over and holds me. "Darling, you're a blessing. I prayed God would give Randi a friend, and you showed up. You were there for her when she needed a friend the most. You made her last days bearable. She told me so. She knew how much you cared for her. She remembered all the good times you shared together. Randi would want you to remember them too." Somehow, Miss Barbara's words and the warmth of her hug comfort me, and I calm down. Maybe God did answer one of my prayers. I just didn't expect the answer to be me.

We miss the turn to the gravesite and get lost, so Dad decides to go straight home. In the car, my nose snorts like hiccups I can't control, so I cover my face with my hands until we pull into the driveway. As soon as Mom opens the front door, I run into my room to change. Even my clothes look like they were crying. I wash my face and try to remove every scent of the funeral.

Sometime later—I lost track of time—there is a knock at the door. I have no idea who it could be, but I answer it. Mr.

Picconi hands me the blue sweater I left behind. "Rita found this on the floor. Hey, that was a quick change. Are you a superhero in disguise?"

I try to stop my eyebrows from scrunching. Does he mean I changed from sad to happy? Does he think I was pretending to cry before? Does he think I don't care about his daughter or that I won't miss her? That I was faking the tears? It doesn't occur to me that he could mean I changed from a dress to pants as fast as Wonder Woman until I walk by the hall mirror. All I want to do is climb into my bed, sleep, and erase this day.

39

Time makes no sense. It races away when I'm on vacation, when I want time to stop. But when I want time to speed up, when there is something I want to forget, time stalls. I'm waiting for the day when I forget I can't go over to Randi's after school. I'm waiting for the day I can look out the window and not imagine her lying on her bed alone that last hour. Will I ever be able to talk to her family without feeling sad or thinking about their sadness, seeing her in their faces? Hartwell Drive will always be the street where a young girl, my friend, died of cancer.

Every morning, I run down the driveway to get the mail. I yank open the mailbox that never worked smoothly after Mr. Picconi hit it, and glance over to Randi's. Every morning since she died, Mr. Picconi sits on their front step, the same step where on hot summer days Randi used to sit and eat her turkey sandwiches on rainbow-colored plastic plates. Now Mr. Picconi sits there, staring straight ahead like he's watching a baseball game on TV—a game that's been delayed from rain. Is he waiting for life to start as he stares all day long from Randi's steps?

A week goes by, and a month. A slow, painful month. I start going to Nina's house more often. She understands why I didn't spend much time with her during Randi's last weeks.

Nina's house is still a great escape from Hartwell Drive, but I'm not hiding from friendship troubles anymore. I'm avoiding memories. Mom drives me over to her house or I ride my bike, and when I'm there, I can laugh again.

Hanging out with Nina doesn't bring back the guilty feelings I would have if I hung out with Isabelle. Isabelle has been nice to me and has invited me over. She must feel sad about Randi, and guilty too, for taking me away from her and for teaming up with Becky, but I still can't go there.

Hartwell Drive is not the same anymore. Around the block, kids play games but not near Randi's house. I don't know if it is out of respect for what the Picconis are going through, for fear of seeing them and not knowing what to say, or because parents told them to keep a distance. There seems to be an invisible fence set to protect and isolate the Picconis' home, letting them grieve alone. I haven't seen Michael outside once since the funeral.

Another month passes, and Hartwell Drive is almost normal again. It's the middle of August. Kids ride bikes in the street, swim in pools, and run through sprinklers. Mr. Picconi doesn't sit on the steps for hours at a time anymore. Instead, he's in constant motion around his lawn. He mows, plants, weeds, and trims until dark. In the evening, he and Mrs. Picconi walk around the block like they used to. Even

Michael is outside playing baseball again. Is their mourning less painful when they are busy?

There's also something new: a *For Sale* sign on the Picconis' lawn. I can't imagine them not living next door, even though I haven't talked with them much since the funeral—just the occasional hello. The Picconis are still our neighbors. No one else could live there.

Mom hangs up the phone. "Mrs. Picconi wants us to come over. She's clearing out her basement and found some things she wants to give us."

"Do I have to? I don't want to go in their house."

"I know it's hard, but you need to stop wondering what it's like in Randi's house. I need to do that too. And I need your help carrying boxes, so let's go."

Mrs. Picconi hugs me at the door. "By the way, I never got a chance to wish you a happy birthday. I can't believe you're a teenager now."

"I can't believe it either," Mom says. "These years go so fast, it seems like yesterday that I was pushing her around in a stroller."

Please stop, Mom, before we all start crying. Mrs. Picconi must be thinking about Randi's stroller days, and that she never got to be a teenager.

We follow Mrs. Picconi down the hall, and I try not to think of Randi, but she's everywhere. I hear her in her den singing along with Billy Joel. I see her sprinkle glitter at the table. I smell her "Bounty fresh" clothes. I go down the basement stairs and feel Randi's soft hands showing me how to run Michael's train set.

"Francie, please get the box I left in the kitchen."

"Sure." I'm glad she didn't ask me to go upstairs. I can't. Walking by the counter, I notice the drawing I made for Randi's birthday card. Someone framed it in pale wood that has the words *Best Friends* printed along each side. *I miss you Randi.*

Mrs. Picconi comes into the kitchen and stands next to me. She puts her arm on my shoulders. "I know," she says.

"Ouch!" Michael's remote control car crashes into my ankles and races away, spoiling the moment. I hear Michael giggle in the other room.

40

It's not the sound of birds chirping that wakes me up today, it's the crashing sound of truck doors slamming. I look out my window and see a moving van that takes up half the street in front of the Picconis' house. They're going to Maryland.

Almost a year has passed since Randi died. Even though the *For Sale* sign sat on their lawn, I didn't believe it would happen. I prayed they would change their minds and stay. God never answered me or explained the "whys," but I think he did sew a patch on my hurting heart. Last Sunday, I actually paid attention in church. I heard how much he loves everyone. That was the first stitch. I realize now that the sign on their lawn and the move are ways to get rid of some of the painful memories. Maybe God will bless them in Maryland to make up for their suffering. Maybe he has other reasons that are too hard for me to understand.

It's Saturday, so I take my time getting ready. Like a magnet, I am pulled to the window to watch the movers take the furniture that created the warm atmosphere in their home and stack it in the truck. I know every piece and where it sat in their house. I can't imagine how their house looks now. *Will I feel worse when strangers move their things into Randi's house—into Randi's room?* The Picconis put everything they owned in the truck, but they couldn't pack their house. Whenever I look over at that house, I will see them and I will see Randi.

I need to say good-bye to the Picconis today, but I don't want to walk into the empty house. All of the memories have been removed, and I have my usual problem—I don't know what to say. The truck is getting fuller, and there's not much time before they leave. I toss clothes on my bed, trying to figure out the right outfit for this cool spring day, and I hear Mom at the front door.

"Hi Guys. Come on in. Would you like some coffee?"

"Thanks, but Sal wants to get an early start. We need to get the last stuff in the car and get going. We just came to say good-bye to our special neighbors."

"We thought we would have another week to get organized, but I got a call from my new company, and they want me to start work on Monday. It's a rush, but I'm excited to work again."

I slip my pants and shirt on, brush my teeth, and run out barefoot. Laurie tags along behind me in her nightgown. Mom is already hugging Mrs. Picconi. The two of them are crying. I walk outside just in time to see Dad hand Mr. Picconi the portrait he did of Randi.

"No! Don't give that away, please?"

Dad turns red and gives me a puzzled look, but I don't care. I remember the day she posed. That drawing is how I want to remember her.

"Come here, Francie." Mrs. Picconi holds her arms out to me. I dissolve into tears as she hugs me tightly. "That's okay. You keep the portrait. She'd want you to."

Mrs. Picconi takes the portrait and hands it to me. "You will always have a place in our hearts. You're a sweet girl. We'll miss you." She places the framed drawing I did for Randi for her birthday on the table along with the journal. "I want you to keep these too. Randi would want you to have them to remind you of your special friendship. She never got to write her story in the journal, but maybe you'll write your own story in it."

I smile and thank her through tears once again.

Mr. Picconi hugs Laurie, and then he hugs me. "We're going to miss our crazy neighbors." It's good to hear him joke again.

We high-five Michael and hug him too. Our good-byes are done. The Picconis walk out our door for the last time.

Then Michael is back. He races through the door for the matchbox car he left on our couch and grabs another hug from Mom. I wonder if he left it on purpose. He waves again with his eyes down, hidden under his Mets baseball cap.

Not long after, I hear a horn honk. We rush outside to wave to the Picconis as they drive off. Maybe this will be the last time that lump strangles my throat. Waving to them makes me think about how I said good-bye to each member of their family, except Randi—the one I knew the best. She moved away forever, and I never got to say it. I guess she knew how I hate good-byes.

Good-bye is an ending, and I hate endings. I hate to finish reading a book. I hate the end of a good movie. I hate the last spoonful of mint chocolate chip ice cream. Maybe we didn't get to say good-bye because it wasn't the end of our friendship.

Randi was taken away too soon—like a glistening bubble blown on a sunny day that pops soon after it rises. But the bubble doesn't just vanish. The water has to go somewhere.

Randi isn't gone. She just leaped off her steps—straight into heaven. I don't know what other steps I'll have to climb, but when I reach the end, I bet Randi will be there, dangling her feet at the top. She'll hand me a slice of angel food cake swirling with extra-thick chocolate frosting and pink flowers. It will be the beginning.

****

In loving memory of my childhood friend.

Acknowledgements

I want to thank my editor, Jeanette Atwood Morris for her insightful, meticulous editing and for encouraging me with praise and prayers. She understood the depth of my emotion poured into this story.

I want to thank my husband, Gene, for listening to my ideas and revisions and giving his honest opinions, for loving me with all my obsessions and crazy writing schedule.

Thank you to my parents and sister, Laurie, for reading my story, helping me with details along the way and encouraging me through the years.

Thank you to my mother-in-law, Clementine, for reading my first draft and sharing her home so I had a place to write.

And I have to thank my dear friend Amy Katz for reading each beginning chapter at Starbucks, for making me laugh and sharing my joys and sorrows.

I thank the many adults and children who read my first edited copy and gave their opinions: Lilly Conforti who gave such great advice, Cheryl Carter, Janae Carter, Paula Servellon, Mary McDonagh, Gigi Van Deckter, Nicky Van Deckter, Eve Hedges, Ali Marshall, Kyla Norton, Sara Martin, Deana Hepner, Kathy Oster, Mara Swanson, and my daughter, Jordan. I will always treasure the time Jordan read *Randi's Steps* out loud to me.

And most of all, I thank my Lord and Savior, Jesus, for being my comfort and providing the peace that passes all understanding.

My heart and prayers go out to all the families who have had to suffer through a time of childhood cancer, especially my cousin, Jenny, and her husband, Reggie, who lost their beautiful four-year-old daughter to brain cancer.